The Eye

"You are the Chieftain of one of the most important Clans in Scotland," said Vara. "Your people
need you and they need you urgently!"

"Then they will have to learn to do without
me," the Earl said perversely.

Vara rose to her feet.

She had started to walk across the room before
he said sharply:

"What are you doing? Where are you going?"

"I am going home," she said. "I can see you
are a hopeless case, and since there is nothing I
can do for you, there is no point in my staying
here . . ."

A Camfield Novel of Love
by Barbara Cartland

———————

Camfield Place,
Hatfield
Hertfordshire,
England

Dearest Reader,

Camfield Novels of Love mark a very exciting era of my books with Jove. They have already published nearly two hundred of my titles since they became my first publisher in America, and now all my original paperback romances in the future will be published exclusively by them.

As you already know, Camfield Place in Hertfordshire is my home, which originally existed in 1275, but was rebuilt in 1867 by the grandfather of Beatrix Potter.

It was here in this lovely house, with the best view in the county, that she wrote *The Tale of Peter Rabbit*. Mr. McGregor's garden is exactly as she described it. The door in the wall that the fat little rabbit could not squeeze underneath and the goldfish pool where the white cat sat twitching its tail are still there.

I had Camfield Place blessed when I came here in 1950 and was so happy with my husband until he died, and now with my children and grandchildren, that I know the atmosphere is filled with love and we have all been very lucky.

It is easy here to write of love and I know you will enjoy the Camfield Novels of Love. Their plots are definitely exciting and the covers very romantic. They come to you, like all my books, with love.

Bless you,

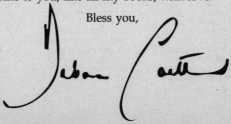

CAMFIELD NOVELS OF LOVE

by Barbara Cartland

A NEW CAMFIELD NOVEL OF LOVE BY

BARBARA CARTLAND

The Eyes of Love

J

JOVE BOOKS, NEW YORK

THE EYES OF LOVE

A Jove Book / published by arrangement with
the author

PRINTING HISTORY
Jove edition / November 1994

ISBN: 0-515-11496-0

A JOVE BOOK®
Jove Books are published by The Berkley Publishing Group,
200 Madison Avenue, New York, New York 10016.
JOVE and the "J" design are trademarks
belonging to Jove Publications, Inc.

PRINTED IN THE UNITED STATES OF AMERICA

10 9 8 7 6 5 4 3 2 1

Author's Note

FROM boyhood, a Highland Chief began to understand, or at least to enjoy, his peculiar position in life. He was of the same blood, name, and descent of his people, but he stood halfway between them and God.

Edward Burt wrote in the eighteenth century:

"The ordinary Highlanders esteem it the most sublime degree of virtue to love their Chief and pay him a blind obedience although it be in opposition to the Government, the laws of the Kingdom, or even the law of God. He is their idol; and as they profess to know no King but him, so will they say they ought to do whatever he commands."

A Chief was not distinguished by the degree of his fortune or by the splendour of his dress, though some walked like peacocks in tartan and silver.

His power and importance rested in the cattle on his braes, and in the number of pretty fellows he could have in his entourage when he went abroad.

Thus did a Macdonald of Keppoch boast that his rent-roll was five hundred fighting-men. In such a climate of pride and sensitive honour the hospitality of the Highlands was more often manifest vanity.

When this same Keppoch was told by a guest of the great candelabra to be seen in the houses of England, he ringed his table with tall clansmen, each holding aloft a flaming pine-knot. Keppoch grinned at his guest.

"Where in England, France, or Italy is there a house with such candlesticks?" he asked.

A Scot is always a Scot, and wherever he goes his instinctive love for "Bonnie Scotland" is always uppermost in his mind and heart.

The Eyes of Love

chapter one

1883

VARA looked out over the bay at the lights on the distant Moors and felt a thrill go through her.

It was wonderful to be back in Scotland.

She told herself there was no place in the world like it.

She had been in England looking after her Aunt, who had sent for her because she was dying.

She took a long time about it, but when she did die, Vara was free to come home.

Her Aunt had left her a thousand pounds in her Will.

"The first thing I will do, Mama," Vara said to her Mother, "is to redecorate the Drawing-Room, and it certainly needs it!"

"You should keep the money for your trousseau," her Mother replied.

Vara laughed.

"I am not thinking of needing one, and I can assure you there were no men about in Aunt Amy's house. It was very quiet there, and at times a little depressing."

"I know, Dearest," Lady McDorn said. "It was very kind of you to go, and you have always been Amy's favourite niece."

Vara could not help thinking that the months she had been away had seemed a long time in the quiet little village in Gloucestershire.

It was where her Aunt had lived ever since she had become a widow.

Her Uncle had been a distinguished man, but his family home, to which he had retired, was in an isolated part of the country.

Anyway, it was now over, and Vara was home, which to her was a delight beyond words.

The McDorns' house was old and had been in the family for many generations.

They were always very proud that they were direct descendants of Robert the Bruce, one of the most exciting Kings of Scotland.

General Sir Alistair McDorn, when he retired from the Army, had only his pension and a modest amount of capital left him by his Father.

This meant that they had to be careful what they spent.

Mr. McDorn had, however, been insistent that their only child, Vara, should have a good education.

She had been educated at home by highly qualified English governesses until she was sixteen.

Then she went to England to what was considered the best Finishing School.

The pupils were mostly daughters of aristocrats and were to make their *début* in London Society.

This was something which was not possible for Vara, but it had not worried her.

She had enjoyed receiving first-class instruction in every subject that interested her.

She was well aware that her Father and Mother had to skimp and save to pay the fees.

That she was at the top of almost every class was their reward.

When she was eighteen she returned home to the Scotland she loved.

She did not regret the festivities that her friends would be enjoying in London.

Only a few months after her return, however, her Aunt had sent for her.

That meant that she had been more or less incarcerated in Gloucestershire until now.

Because she was so excited to be back, she wanted to run to the end of the garden which led straight onto the beach.

Golden sand edged the bay, and above it were the Moors, purple with heather.

The lights she had missed in England changed hour by hour, each one seeming more lovely than the last.

"There is so much I want to see now that I am home," she murmured.

Her Mother was working on a tapestry which she was making for a chair cover.

"I am delighted, my Darling," she said, "to have you back. At the same time, you may now find it very dull."

"It could never be dull here," Vara replied, "and this afternoon I am going to climb to the top of our Moor and watch as the river runs into the sea."

It was something she had loved doing as a small child, and Lady McDorn laughed.

"You used to make me tell you stories," she reminded her, "of how you sailed away on the river to distant lands."

"I have been to them all, in my mind," Vara declared, "but I have decided that I would rather be at home in Scotland than anywhere else in the world!"

"That is what I want you to say, Darling," Lady McDorn answered, "but I wish there were a few more people here of your age. Perhaps when the new Earl is better, he will give a party."

"The Earl?" Vara questioned. "Is he home?"

"I thought I mentioned it when I last wrote to you," Lady McDorn replied. "He has come back from India, but his eyes are affected."

"Do you mean he was wounded?" Vara asked.

"I do not think so," Lady McDorn said, "but somebody told me that his eyes were bandaged when he arrived about seven days ago. We have heard nothing more since."

Vara thought this was strange.

The knowledge that the Earl of Dornoch, the Chieftain of the McDorns, was home would certainly excite the Clan.

What made it even more interesting was that he was someone they did not know.

Vara supposed there had been a gathering to greet him on his arrival.

Soon there would be the ceremony at which the Clansmen, one by one, pledged their allegiance to him.

"If he is home, Mama," she said, "surely you and Papa should have called on him by now?"

"That, of course, is what we intended to do," Lady McDorn answered, "but we were told that because his eyes are afflicted, he will see nobody."

"See nobody?" Vara repeated. "How extraordinary! But perhaps he is in pain."

She thought that if that was the case, the

Doctors would be attending him.

Before her Mother could answer the questions that came to her mind, the door of the Drawing-Room opened.

The General came in, accompanied by the Minister.

The latter was an elderly man who had known Vara since she was a child.

"I heard you were home, Vara," the Minister said as she moved towards him, "and it is very good to have you back."

"I am so happy to be here," Vara answered. "Mama was just beginning to tell me all the news. It is very exciting that the Earl is in the Castle."

"That is exactly what I came to see you about, my child," the Minister said, "but let me first greet your Mother."

He walked to Lady McDorn's chair. She did not rise because she suffered with arthritis.

"You must forgive me for not coming to the Kirk this Sunday," she said, "but I had a bad night, and Alistair insisted that I stay at home."

"He was quite right to do so," the Minister said. "But I missed you, and I have missed little Vara while she has been away."

He smiled at Vara as he spoke, then said:

"I have come here on a strange mission, but I think, when you hear what I have to say, you will realise that it is an important one."

"Let me first offer you some refreshment," the General said. "Will you join me in a glass of sherry?"

"I would be delighted," the Minister replied.

The General went from the room, and the Minister sat down on a sofa.

"What I have come to tell you," he said, addressing Vara, "is that the new Earl is in a bad way."

"Mama was telling me that his eyes are afflicted. But what happened?" Vara asked. "Was he injured in a battle?"

"No one knows when the actual injury occurred," the Minister said, "but the fact is that he cannot see. The Doctors have forbidden him to try to use his eyes. He has to keep them bandaged for at least two months."

"Did this happen in India?" Vara asked.

"I think it happened when he was on the North-West Frontier," the Minister replied, "but he is reluctant to speak about it, and he is making things very difficult for everybody at the Castle."

Lady McDorn looked up from her embroidery.

"I did hear a rumour that something was wrong," she said, "but I thought it best not to speak about it."

"You were quite right," the Minister said. "What we want is that the Earl should realise the importance of his position as Chieftain of the Clan, and settle down happily at the Castle, which at the moment apparently is not happening."

"But why?" Vara asked. "Is it because he cannot see?"

"I think that is the main reason," the Minister said, "but he is making life difficult for everybody. He is even refusing to receive the Elders of the Clan."

Vara looked astonished.

She knew this was something which would deeply upset the Elders, who were very conscious of their importance.

If they were dissatisfied with their new Chieftain, it would gradually affect the McDorns wherever they might be.

"What can you do about it?" Vara asked.

"That is exactly why I have come here this morning," the Minister answered. "I was approached by His Lordship's Secretary, Mr. Bryden, whom I am sure you remember, and who has been at the Castle for over twenty years."

"Of course I remember him," Vara agreed.

"He feels that something must be done for His Lordship, and the most important thing is for him to have a Reader."

"Surely, Mr. Bry—" Lady McDorn began.

The Minister held up his hand.

"I am just going to explain. Mr. Bryden tells me the Earl cannot understand the Scottish accent. He insisted on having someone who speaks the same sort of English that he does."

Vara gave a little gasp.

"He does not understand the Scottish accent?" she exclaimed. "But . . . he is a Scot!"

"Indeed he is, or he would not be the ninth Earl of Dornoch!" the Minister replied. "But he was brought up as an Englishman."

He paused and then continued:

"His Father, who had married the daughter of an English nobleman, had not supposed it was at all likely that he or his son would ever succeed to the Earldom."

Vara remembered that the late Earl had only one son.

He had been in the Black Watch and had been posted to the Sudan under Major General Gordon.

Vara could remember how devastated the Clan had been when the Viscount's body had been brought back home and placed in the family vault in the Kirk.

In Scotland, at any rate, the Earl of Dornoch was of great importance.

Any disparagement of the Scots by the new Earl would be received with horror and deep resentment.

"You will understand," the Minister went on, "that because the last Earl was so ill for a long time before he died, there was much left undone that should now be put in hand, including repairs to the Castle itself. The only person who can give the orders for this to be carried out is, of course, His Lordship."

"And he refuses?" Vara asked.

"I am afraid he cannot, or will not, understand the particulars when they are read to him by Mr. Bryden, or by anybody else in the Castle."

"They must feel deeply offended by that!" Vara said in a low voice.

"It is something which, if talked about outside, could do him a great deal of damage," the Minister said. "Everybody has been looking forward to having a young Chieftain with new ideas, who will encourage and initiate new local industry."

Vara was well aware that this was true.

Like most of the ordinary people of Scotland, the McDorns relied on their spinning and their fishing to earn money on which to live.

They thought of their Chieftain not only as their Leader, but as their Shepherd.

To them he was a Father-figure who would inspire and comfort them.

The idea of the Earl being too English even to understand their speech would strike them a blow.

Vara knew it would be difficult for them to accept it.

"What can you do about it?" she asked the Minister.

"The answer to that, Vara, is what will *you* do about it?"

"Me?" Vara enquired.

"Mr. Bryden wants someone who can read to His Lordship in an English accent, but there is no-one here who is capable of doing that except yourself."

Vara's eyes widened, but she knew the Minister was speaking the truth.

Like most upper-class children, even of Scots blood, she had been brought up to speak with an English accent, and had completed her education in England.

There was silence until she said:

"Are you really asking me to go to the Castle and read to His Lordship?"

"I am begging you to do so," the Minister answered. "Mr. Bryden has been very loyal and has kept people who are curious away from him. At the same time, he says he dare not let the Fishermen, the Game-Keepers, the Gillies, or anyone else near His Lordship because he will undoubtedly tell them that he cannot understand what they are saying."

"And obviously has no wish to do so," Vara remarked. "It seems to me he is a very spoilt young man, and somebody should warn him what harm he can do if he continues to behave in such a ridiculous manner."

"I doubt if what you are suggesting would do any good," the Minister answered. "He seems most reluctant to accept the position in which he finds himself, and deeply resents that he cannot see. At the same time, he hates offers of pity or sympathy because, I think, he finds them degrading."

Lady McDorn sighed.

"I can see your problem, Minister."

"I have a feeling," the Minister said, "that it could be solved if Vara, who has always been a very clever girl, could not only read to him, but try to impress upon him that the Clan really needs his leadership."

Vara knew this was true.

The last Earl had been over eighty when he died.

For the last five years he had been completely senile.

No-one had seen him except the Minister and the Doctors, who admitted they could do nothing for him.

Vara knew her Father had commiserated with the Elders.

Everything they said was going to rack and ruin without their Chieftain to inspire and direct them.

She had often thought when she was in England that the Scots were very childlike in many ways.

They relied on their Chieftain to solve every problem for them.

She did not stop to think over what the Minister had asked of her, but said without hesitating:

"Of course, if I can do any good, I will come to the Castle. Would you like to take me back with you?"

"If it is not asking too much," the Minister replied. "I think it would be most helpful if you would stay at the Castle for a few days."

"Stay there?" Vara questioned. "But why?"

"Mr. Bryden tells me that because His Lordship is in darkness, he does not know night from day. Mr. Bryden is not a young man, and he is often called from his bed to answer some question that is puzzling the Earl, or to read something to him he has not understood."

"Oh, poor Mr. Bryden!" Vara sympathised. "He is far too old to be woken up in the middle of the night."

"That is what I think," the Minister agreed, "and Donald, His Lordship's personal servant, is also beginning to feel the strain."

"Well, I shall certainly tell His Lordship that I need my 'Beauty Sleep,'" Vara said firmly, "and if he is too selfish and inconsiderate I shall disconnect the bells when no-one is looking!"

The Minister laughed, while Lady McDorn said:

"Darling, you must try to understand that for a young man it is intolerable to be blind. I am sure he wants to be catching salmon in the river and shooting on the Moors."

"If he *wants* to get well, that will be half the battle!" Vara answered.

She looked at the Minister and asked:

"What do the Doctors say are the chances of his regaining his sight?"

"I talked to Dr. Adair," the Minister said, "who has the reports from the Specialists in London. He told me the Earl's case is a very strange one."

"Strange? In what way?" Vara asked.

"Well, apparently they cannot find anything wrong with his eyes. It is just that the Earl cannot see!"

"But there obviously is something wrong," Vara said.

"If you ask me," Lady McDorn chipped in, "I think most Doctors are very much behind the times. I am always reading in the newspapers of operations that have gone wrong, and it is obvious that men who are wounded in battle are not treated in the way they should be."

"I agree with you," the Minister replied, "but I suppose medical science does its best."

"I should not be surprised," Lady McDorn

went on, "if the good Scottish air and proper food does not cure him better than anything else."

"I can only hope you are right," the Minister sighed. "In the meantime, you must forgive me for stealing away your daughter when she has just come home. But I know that you will understand."

"Nothing," Vara chimed in, "is more important than to make the new Chieftain behave himself."

The Minister laughed.

Then he said:

"That is not the way I would express it myself, but I agree that it is something very important at this moment."

Vara got to her feet.

"I will go and pack the things I will need," she said, "but I do not promise to stay long. I have been so looking forward to being back here with Papa and Mama."

"Of course you have, my child," the Minister said. "I hate to be a nuisance, but there was no-one else to whom I could turn."

"I will tell you one thing," Vara said as she reached the door, "there are some fine horses in the stables at the Castle, and unless someone has removed them, I shall find them very enjoyable when I am off duty."

The Minister's eyes twinkled.

"I am sure you are right, Vara, and they need

exercise. It would not take you long to ride home to see your Father and Mother."

"That is exactly what I was thinking," Vara said, "and if His Lordship says in English that I am not to do so, that is something I shall certainly not be able to understand!"

The Minister laughed again as she shut the door, and then ran up the stairs.

She could not help thinking that it was an adventure to be going to the Castle as a guest rather than just as a visitor.

Even before she had left home to go to England, her Father and Mother had ceased to visit the old Earl.

If they had done so, he would not have recognised them.

Ever since she was small she had thought the Castle was exciting, if rather frightening.

Standing firm, overlooking the bay, the Castle had repelled the Vikings when they invaded Scotland from the other side of the North Sea.

According to the History-Books, the Clansmen had proved so ferocious that the land belonging to the McDorns had been left untouched.

Farther North the Picts had taken refuge in caves and hid until the Viking ships had left, carrying off sheep and cattle.

They had also left a legacy behind them of fair-haired children with blue eyes, whose descendants, so many generations later, looked remarkably like the Vikings.

The Earls of Dornoch had inspired their Clan to fight ferociously to preserve their women and their possessions.

This was the reason the Clan had been respected all down the centuries.

They were reputed to hold their heads higher than any of their neighbours.

"Surely the new Earl must be aware of this?" Vara asked herself.

She packed quickly what she required.

Before she had left England she had bought some very pretty gowns with the money left her by her Aunt.

She had not been extravagant.

At the same time, she knew that her Father and Mother would like her to look her best.

So she did not feel it was wrong to spend a little of the money on herself.

She felt she had earned it over the months during which she had nursed her Aunt.

There would be no-one at the Castle, however, she thought wistfully, to see her in her elegant gowns she had bought to wear at dinner.

She changed into a dress in a pale shade of blue with a short jacket, in which to travel to the Castle.

The hat that went with it had been bought in Bond Street.

Her Cousin with whom she had stayed in

London for a few days before travelling home had told her it was exceedingly becoming.

"You should stay with us, Vara dear," she said. "I know of some charming young men who would love to meet you."

"I must go home to Papa and Mama," Vara replied, "but, please, ask me again in a month or so, because there is so much I want to see in London."

"You shall see everything!" the Cousin promised. "Just tell me when you have had enough of the purple heather, and your bedroom here will be waiting for you."

Vara had kissed her Cousin.

On her way North she thought it would be very exciting to spend a few weeks in London.

She wanted to go to the Theatres and the Opera and, most important of all, to a Ball.

The girls at School had talked about their "Coming Out" Balls and the numerous parties to which they had been invited.

They all had a special ambition, to be invited to Marlborough House.

Edward, Prince of Wales, and his love-affairs with lovely women like Lillie Langtry, were whispered about at the School.

Vara, like many of her friends, could not help wondering if she would ever be beautiful enough to attract a Prince.

She told herself it was certainly something

that would not happen as long as she was in Scotland.

There the Princes were few and far between, unless one was lucky enough to live in Edinburgh, where the Duke of Hamilton entertained Royal guests.

At the same time, Vara was not, like some of the girls, intent on being admired and pursued by men.

She found so much other interest in the various subjects she had studied.

Books had revealed to her a very different world from the one in which she lived.

At the moment, every day was a new adventure with something she might learn, or something to discover.

She reflected as she finished her packing that when she had come home, looking forward to being with her Father and Mother, she had never imagined that anything like this would happen to her.

She went down the stairs to find her Father and the Minister each with a glass of sherry in his hand.

Her Mother was saying:

"Is it really correct for Vara to stay at the Castle without a Chaperon?"

"I have thought of that," the Minister answered, "but have you forgotten—Mrs. Bryden is there."

"Of course," Lady McDorn said, "how foolish

of me! But she is such a retiring woman that I always think of Mr. Bryden as a bachelor."

The Minister smiled.

"Many people make that mistake, but Mrs. Bryden likes being alone, and she was determined that her rooms at the Castle should be inviolate."

They all laughed.

They knew the story of how Mr. Bryden, as a young man, had approached the old Earl when he wished to be married.

He had then been informed that it was absolutely forbidden in any circumstances for him to live outside the Castle.

"I need you and I want you here with me," the Earl had said.

He could be very ferocious when he wished, and definitely intimidating.

Mr. Bryden, however, had stood his ground.

"I am sorry, M'Lord, if this means I have to leave your service."

"Leave my service?" the Earl thundered. "I have never heard such damned nonsense! Of course you cannot leave my service! I trust you and you suit me. You will stay here if I have to lock you up in one of the dungeons!"

Mr. Bryden had laughed, and capitulated.

"I intend to be married, M'Lord," he said, "but if it doesn't suit you that I should have a cottage on the Estate, which is what I had hoped for, I could perhaps have one of the towers for myself and my future wife."

The Earl considered this for a moment, then agreed.

There were four towers, one at each corner of the Castle.

The rooms within them each rose to one storey, but they could be made very comfortable and certainly provided a picturesque and original home.

Mrs. Bryden, who was a local woman of over thirty, had accepted the situation because there was no alternative.

She, however, made it perfectly clear that her home was her own and intruders were barred.

Mr. Bryden had therefore continued as Secretary to the Earl, which meant he coped with everything, the Estate as well as the Castle.

Because his wife was so retiring and her Tower was certainly *her* Castle, it was easy for most people to forget she existed.

"Yes, of course Mrs. Bryden is there," Lady McDorn said, "and I am sure, Dearest Vara, should you need any advice or help, she will help you as best she can."

"I shall be all right, Mama. Do not worry about me," Vara said, "and I have every intention of riding home every day to tell you what is happening."

"You will have to ask His Lordship's permission first," Lady McDorn warned her.

She spoke a little anxiously because there was a glint in her daughter's eye which told her that Vara intended to get her own way.

She had a strong determination which she had inherited from her Father.

The General had had a reputation when he was in the Army of winning every battle in which he was engaged.

The reason was that he never knew when he was beaten.

Even as a very small child, Vara had shown her determination.

As her Mother had once said:

"You can persuade her by love, but never by force."

Now, as Lady McDorn looked at her daughter, she thought that, even in the months during which she had been away, Vara had grown more beautiful.

Her fair hair with just a touch of red in it accentuated the whiteness of her skin.

She never seemed to burn with the sun.

Her eyes were very large, green with a touch of gold in them.

They seemed to fill her small, pointed face, so that anyone meeting her remembered her eyes more than anything else about her.

'She is really beautiful!' Lady McDorn

thought, and could not help feeling it was a pity that the Earl would not be able to see her.

Then she told herself severely that this was no time for match-making.

Anyway it was extremely unlikely that the Earl of Dornoch would be interested in a local girl of Scottish descent.

'I expect,' she thought, 'that as soon as he can see again, he will be off to London, like so many of the young Chieftains to-day who neglect their duty to their Clans because they find the big City more alluring than the moors.'

It had been a subject for condemnation all through the last century.

It was, of course, understandable that the young Scottish Chieftains wanted to enjoy themselves and be with their contemporaries.

They found it more fun than dealing with local difficulties and problems.

Yet Clansmen relied on them to the point where they hardly thought for themselves.

Vara was aware how much the McDorns had been looking forward to having a new Chieftain, and how disappointed they must be.

"Do your best, Darling," her Mother said, "and, of course, if you want us at any time, your Father and I will come and help in any way we can."

"I know you will do that, Mama," Vara replied, "but if the Earl thinks my English accent is not good enough for him, I may return home to-morrow morning!"

"If that happens," the Minister said, "His Lordship will have to talk to the gulls, for there is no-one else I can turn to on his behalf."

"I am sure, Minister," Lady McDorn said, "that Vara will do what you ask very successfully."

She had risen painfully to her feet, and shook hands with the Minister.

Then she put her arms round her daughter and held her close.

"Take care of yourself, my Darling. Your Father and I will be counting the days until you come back to us."

Vara kissed her Mother.

"I will be over to see you to-morrow," she promised, "come hell or high water!"

Feeling perhaps she had been indiscreet in front of the Minister, she turned to look at him.

He was smiling.

"Come along, Vara" was all he said. "It may not be as difficult as you think, and you will certainly be taking a great deal of weight off my shoulders."

The General accompanied them to the door.

The Minister's carriage was an old one drawn by a horse that was too fat to move very fast.

A groom was holding its head, although it had no intention of moving.

As the Minister picked up the reins, he said:

"Thank you, Ewen. You have been very helpful."

"If you ask me, Minister," the General remarked, "you feed that horse too well!"

"I expect you are right," the Minister agreed, "but when she tells me she is hungry, I do not like to refuse her."

The old groom, who had been with the Minister for years, grinned.

"Ye dinna say that, Sir," he said, "when us drink too much at a Funeral!"

The Minister shook his head and did not reply.

He had complained that after Funerals, which in Scotland were attended only by men, the mourners were often so drunk on secretly distilled whisky that they could not find their way home.

The groom touched his cap.

Vara waved as the Minister drove his carriage away from the front-door.

She looked back to see her Father and Mother standing on the steps of the house.

She thought they were looking a little forlorn.

'They mind my leaving them,' she told herself. 'But Papa knows that I must do what I can to help the Clan.'

She waved until she could see them no longer.

She then settled down comfortably to enjoy the drive over the high road which would eventually take them to the Castle.

chapter two

THEY drove for a little while in silence.

Then Vara said:

"You had better tell me exactly what the new Earl's position is in the family. I had never heard of him until my Mother told me he was here."

"The story is a little complicated," the Minister answered. "The old Earl had two brothers; the elder, James, was a very strange man who was almost a recluse and died unmarried."

He paused and adjusted his reins before he went on:

"The second brother, Hector, was born in Scotland and married a Scottish girl. But they went South to live in England, and had one son, Malcolm, who was the Father of the present Earl."

Vara thought for a moment.

Then she said:

"That makes him a great-nephew of the old Earl."

"That is correct," the Minister agreed. "After the child was born, whose name is Bruce, his Father and Mother separated. Malcolm McDorn went abroad, travelling to far-distant countries, until he died when still only in middle-age."

"How did he die?" Vara asked.

"He caught some obscure fever in Africa, and that is where he is buried."

"They do not sound a very affectionate family," Vara remarked.

"Malcolm had married into an old and respected English family, the Lancasters," the Minister said. "His Father-in-law was a Marquess, and his son was brought up by the Lancasters in an entirely English fashion."

Vara was listening with interest as the Minister continued:

"Bruce went to Eton and Oxford, and then, completely ignoring the fact that the McDorns have always served in the Black Watch, joined the Household Cavalry."

"So I suppose he can ride well!" Vara murmured.

"He went to India last year," the Minister went on, "as *Aide-de-Camp* to the Viceroy—the Marquess of Ripon."

"So he was not on active service as a soldier, which I thought was how he lost his eyesight," Vara said. "Papa said he was on the North-West Frontier."

"I think he was," the Minister answered somewhat vaguely. "But he was attending the Viceroy."

Vara thought she would have respected him more if he had been fighting in battle against the Afghan tribesmen.

She had always been told that they were incited to rebel by the Russians and armed by them.

"How old is the present Earl?" she asked when they had gone a little further.

"He will be twenty-eight next birthday," the Minister replied, "and I think he would be an intelligent and most charming man if he was not so sensitive about his affliction and, as far as I can make out, actually resentful at becoming Chieftain of the Clan."

"Then why did he come here if he feels like that?" Vara asked.

The Minister thought for a moment.

Then he said:

"It is a question I asked myself, and I think

the answer is that he did not want his friends in London to see him blinded. I imagine also that, when the news of the late Earl's death reached him in India and he knew he was his heir, pressure must have been put on him to come to Scotland."

Vara could understand that.

She agreed also that it was a convenient hiding place because he had no wish for anyone to see him incapacitated.

They drove on, the Minister's horse getting slower as they went up a hill.

Finally, they descended towards the Castle which Vara could see in the distance.

Its towers and spires were very impressive.

As Vara knew, however, it looked its most formidable when seen from the sea.

Then it stood in the centre of the bay, defying its enemies.

At that moment, with the sun shining on a smooth sea and the lights glinting on the Moors, she thought nothing could be more beautiful.

"But of course, if the Earl cannot see it, he does not know what he is missing," she told herself practically.

Finally, when they drove in at the great gates and down the tree-bordered drive, the Castle at the end of it seemed enormous and at the same time it looked mysterious.

Because Vara had first come to the Castle as a child, it had always been in the background of her thoughts as a place which was strange, ghostly, and altogether overwhelming.

Now, she told herself, it would be impossible for any man, if he could see the Castle, not to be proud of the fact that it was his heritage.

It went back into history to the eleventh century.

The Minister drew his horse to a standstill outside the front-door, which had a flight of stone steps leading up to it.

On either side of them stood a stone emblem of a wild cat, which was a feature of the coat-of-arms of the McDorns.

Two servants wearing kilts came hurrying out to open the doors of the carriage.

As Vara stepped out, they greeted her.

She knew a great number of the Clan by sight and by name.

Naturally they all knew her because she had lived in the neighbourhood ever since she was born.

"Where is His Lordship?" the Minister asked as he joined Vara on the steps.

"He's awa' in th' Chieftain's Room, Sir," one of the footmen replied.

He spoke with a very broad Scottish accent.

Vara thought she could understand the Earl finding it difficult to comprehend.

A great number of the McDorns still spoke Gaelic.

She thought that would be an even bigger stumbling-block.

They passed through the hall and walked up the wide staircase.

As in all Scottish Castles, the main rooms were on the First Floor.

Vara knew most of them looked out over the garden directly below, beyond which was a strip of land that led down to the beach.

When they reached the landing, the footman, who had walked ahead of them up the stairs, opened the door into the Chieftain's Room.

It was a very attractive room which Vara knew well.

The walls on one side were lined with books.

All round the walls, just below the ceiling, were mounted the horns of stags.

They had been shot by each succeeding Earl, and every one was a Royal.

Above the huge mantelpiece there was a portrait of the eighth Earl, who had been very handsome, besides being the most important man in Scotland.

Every succeeding Earl had been painted during his lifetime.

They looked down at their present descendant, who was seated in a high-backed chair beside the fireplace.

The Minister and Vara walked towards him.

As they did so, Vara saw that he was wearing English clothes, not, as everybody would have expected, the kilt.

That, if nothing else, she knew, would be considered by the Clan to be an insult.

As she drew nearer, she saw his eyes were bandaged.

At the same time, she thought he was good-looking, broad-shouldered, and taller than she had expected.

He was sitting back in his chair in what she was sure was a despondent attitude.

It was, however, difficult to judge what his thoughts and feelings were with the bandages covering his eyes.

Without being told, the footman announced them.

"Th' Minister, M'Lord," he said, "an' Miss Var-ra McDor-rn."

As they reached the Earl, Vara thought he might have stood up.

Instead, he said in a sharp voice:

"Who is that with you, Minister?"

"I have brought you a Reader, My Lord," the Minister replied. "That is what you wanted, and I think you will find her an exceptionally intelligent young woman. In fact, I have been very fortunate in being able to persuade her to come to you."

The Minister spoke almost aggressively, as if he were determined to make the Earl realise how privileged he was.

The Earl merely said in a somewhat surly tone:

"I hope your protégée, Minister, can speak a language I understand."

"You must judge that for yourself," the Minister said. "Let me introduce Miss Vara McDorn. Her Father, General Sir Alistair McDorn, is one of the most respected and admired members of the Clan."

"That is a very nice introduction," Vara said before the Earl could speak, "and if I ever want a reference in the future, I shall know to whom I can apply!"

She spoke with a hint of laughter in her voice.

If the Earl was listening, he would be aware that she spoke without a trace of a Scottish accent.

There was a short pause.

Then the Earl said:

"You certainly speak English, and thank God for that!"

Vara was about to reply, but the Minister said hastily:

"As I have two calls to make before I can return home, I will leave you now, Vara. I hope that you and His Lordship will become acquainted and that I shall find things very much happier when I call to-morrow."

Although the Earl could not see him, he gave him a respectful bow before he added:

"Good-bye, My Lord. I am sure you will be extremely grateful to Miss McDorn for coming here at such short notice, but she knows how important it is for you to be happy in your new position."

When he finished speaking, he walked away.

He put his hand for a moment on Vara's shoulder in an affectionate gesture, before he left the room.

The Earl did not reply, and Vara sat down on a chair opposite him.

"You will have to tell me," she said, making her voice soft and ingratiating, "exactly what you require and what interests you."

She paused for a moment before she went on:

"I expect you know that the newspapers which come from the South are sometimes delayed, but those from Edinburgh arrive the day after they are published."

"Nothing would surprise me about this place!" the Earl retorted. "Although of course I had heard of the Castle in this isolated part of Scotland, I have never before crossed the Border."

"Then, of course, it is Fate that you should be here, and of special importance at this particular moment."

"What do you mean by 'at this particular moment'?" the Earl enquired.

"You must be aware that the late Earl, your Great-Uncle, was not capable of coping with anything for at least three to four years before he died," Vara answered. "Therefore, because nothing can happen without the approval of the Chieftain, everything has more or less come to a standstill."

"Surely that is a ridiculous state of affairs," the Earl remarked.

"Not for the Scots," Vara replied. "And that is why, now that you are here, there is a great deal to be done."

"How do you think I am going to do it if I cannot see?"

There was no doubt now that the Earl's voice was aggressive.

"That is why I am here," Vara answered. "I will explain to you what is required, and I am sure you will find it easy to make a decision if it is all described to you in detail."

"You are taking on a great deal," the Earl said sharply. "I find it impossible to live as I am now, without being able to see, in perpetual darkness, and, as far as I can make out, with little chance of ever seeing again in the future."

"Are you sure about that?" Vara enquired. "I was told by the Minister that the Doctors found it difficult to diagnose what is wrong with your eyes. It was not suggested that you would never see again."

"I do not wish to discuss it," the Earl said angrily. "I loathe and detest being helpless. If you can find anything to interest me in this 'back of beyond' part of the world, I shall be very surprised!"

"As you have never seen what you call this 'back of beyond' part of the world," Vara pointed out, "do you not think it is rather unfair to judge it, except with your brain and your intelligence?"

She knew from the way the Earl stiffened that she had surprised him.

After a distinctive silence he said:

"I do not know exactly what you mean by that."

Vara settled herself more comfortably in her chair before she replied:

"You do understand that this is your Kingdom? In Scotland everything revolves around the Chieftain. He is King to his particular Clan. What is more, he not only rules, he also protects them, leads, and inspires them. That is what your people are waiting for now."

"Then they will obviously have to wait!" the Earl said. "How can I possibly perform all that nonsense you have just talked about if I cannot see?"

"You can listen with your ears, think with

your mind, and answer with your lips," Vara answered.

She spoke without considering her language because she thought the Earl was being deliberately, almost inexcusably, difficult.

He did not speak, and she went on:

"A Scot, if he has the right blood in him, will never be defeated. He will fight battle after battle against overwhelming odds, where other men of other nationalities would give in. Surely you cannot be the exception?"

There was silence.

Then the Earl said:

"I am wondering to myself what sort of Reader you are. Quite frankly, I have never been spoken to like this before!"

Vara gave a little laugh.

"I am sorry," she said, "I am trying not to be rude, but on my way here I saw the Castle looking so beautiful on the bay. As I drew nearer I thought how strong and stalwart it was, and how it had defied the Vikings. I cannot believe that any McDorn would give way to just a small infirmity."

"Small?" the Earl exclaimed. "You may think that being blind is a 'small' infirmity, but as far as I am concerned, it is nothing short of hell on earth!"

"Then it is something you have to get the better of," Vara said, "and I am certain the last thing you should do is give way to despondency."

She drew in her breath before she added:

"To get well and to be able to see again, you have to *believe* it will happen!"

There was silence.

Then the Earl said:

"And suppose it does not?"

Vara did not answer for a moment.

Then she said:

"I expect you know that all Scots are 'fey.' I am convinced, now that I have seen you, that somehow, sometime, you will regain your sight."

"I suspect you are just trying to encourage me," the Earl said.

"Why should I do that?" Vara asked. "As it happens, I always tell the truth, and I certainly would not lie in making anything like a prediction. It would be most unlucky, not only for the person to whom I am speaking, but also for myself."

There was a faint twist to the Earl's lips as he said:

"Now I come to think of it, I have always been told that the Scots and their country are full of superstitions."

"That is true, but you should say 'My country,'" Vara corrected him. "After all, you are a Scot, and therefore everything you say and think is of importance to the people around you."

"Now you are back again harping on the Clan," the Earl complained. "I have heard nothing else ever since I arrived. I am told that some strange people called the 'Elders of the Clan' wish to see me. There are innumerable McDorns knocking on the door, when all I want is to be left alone!"

"That, I am afraid, is the one thing you cannot be," Vara replied.

"Why not?"

"Because you are the Chieftain of one of the most important Clans in Scotland. Your people need you and they need you urgently!"

"Then they will have to learn to do without me," the Earl said perversely.

Vara rose to her feet.

She had started to walk across the room before he said sharply:

"What are you doing? Where are you going?"

"I am going home," she said. "I can see you are a hopeless case, and since there is nothing I can do for you, there is no point in my staying here."

The Earl made a sound that was almost a shout.

"You are not to leave me," he protested. "I want to talk to you. You are the one person I have been able to understand since I came to this blighted place."

There was a pause, and as Vara did not speak, he said:

"I suppose, in the light of what you have been saying about my manners, I cannot order you to stay."

"Of course you can," Vara answered. "And that at least is a step in the right direction towards showing your authority."

"Very well," the Earl said. "I order you to sit down and listen to me."

Vara was smiling as she went back to the chair in which she had been sitting.

"I will make a deal with you," the Earl said. "You shall tell me what to do, and I will try to behave as you want me to for a week."

He paused for a moment before he went on:

"If, at the end of that time, I find it completely and absolutely impossible, and there is no chance of my regaining my sight, I think I will drown myself in the bay or throw myself off one of the towers. But I cannot go on living forever in this damned darkness."

There was a note of anguish in his voice to which Vara felt herself respond.

Aloud she said:

"Very well, My Lord, I will stay for one week. But you have committed yourself to doing what I want you to do."

"I think I must be mad!" the Earl said in a very different tone. "But I suppose there is just a sporting chance that you may be right, and I shall be able to see again."

"I am sure you will be able to, but I cannot tell you when, and more important than anything else," Vara said, "is that you *believe* that your sight will be restored to you, and you will be able to see as well as you did before you went blind."

Now her voice was very soft and quiet.

The Earl listened almost as if he were hypnotised by it.

He put out his hand.

"I have given you one week," he said.

Vara felt his fingers close over hers.

She was aware that he was very much stronger in character and personality than he pretended to be.

When she sensed the vibrations of the people she met, she never made a mistake.

She knew exactly what they were like and of what they were capable.

She could feel that the Earl could be a great man if he forgot his infirmity and the prejudices with which he had been brought up.

She knew they were a weakness in the position in which he now found himself.

As she took her hand from his, she said:

"May I suggest that the first thing you do, My Lord, is to dress the part? No Chieftain of the McDorns is ever seen on his own territory not wearing the kilt."

There was silence.

She knew that if she could have seen the Earl's eyes, he would have been staring at her.

After a moment he said:

"I never thought of that. But of course I do not possess one."

"I feel sure that Donald, who has been a senior servant here for years, could provide you with one at a moment's notice. Also, you need the sporran and the full dress with the plaid, a cairngorm, and a skean-dhu."

The Earl laughed.

" 'In for a penny, in for a pound.' You can produce the whole fancy-dress, and if I make a clown of myself, I only hope the audience will appreciate the effort I am making on their behalf."

"I can assure you," Vara answered, "that they will not only appreciate you, but will know their hopes have been realised. They have been longing to have a Chieftain who is young, with new ideas, and who will put right everything that has gone wrong since your Great-Uncle became incapable of giving orders."

"Bryden has already told me," the Earl said, "that there are a number of things for me to decide, but I refused to be interested."

"I will find out what they are," Vara said, "then I will read them to you and explain their importance, ranging from the fact that the roof is caving in down to the plaintive cries from the

Kitchen that a new stove is needed."

The Minister had told her this as they were driving along the road.

"Why does not Mr. Bryden order a new one?" she had asked.

"He is afraid that the new Earl would resent his purchasing anything for which he had not given his personal consent."

Vara had smiled because she knew it was the way all the Clan behaved where their Chieftain was concerned.

At the same time, she thought that Mr. Bryden was being foolish and over-sensitive about the Earl.

Now, looking at him, she thought she could understand.

There was a strength about him which made him stand out as a leader of men.

It would certainly discourage them from taking matters into their own hands or making decisions which later the Earl might challenge.

"I will make a list for you," she said now, "and you do understand that one word from you will set the machinery in operation."

She stopped speaking for a moment, and looked at him before continuing:

"Everything here is dependent on the Castle, and, once that is running smoothly, you will have to reach out to the hamlets, the river, and the Moors. In fact, all over the twenty thousand acres you own and rule over in Scotland."

"As much as that?" the Earl exclaimed. "Good Lord, I had no idea it was so large!"

"Most of it is just moorland," Vara said. "There are a number of fishing-villages which I am sure will need your direction, and of course the people themselves. The McDorns want to get to know you, as you must get to know them."

"But as I cannot understand a single word they say," the Earl complained, "it is going to be difficult."

"You will soon learn to understand them," Vara said, "and I think it would be useful if you learned Gaelic."

The Earl raised his hands in dismay.

"That is something I never expected," he said. "I only just managed to assimilate a smattering of Urdu, but Gaelic—it never occurred to me!"

"As you are 'Monarch of all you *cannot* survey,'" Vara misquoted, "there are a great number of things which will surprise you, and I do not mind betting that by the end of the week you will find everything quite interesting, and even exciting."

"You are certainly different from what I expected," the Earl said after a moment's silence. "Tell me what you look like."

Vara laughed.

"I will leave you to guess whether I am a thick-set, sturdy Scotswoman who can walk the Moors untiringly for hours on end, or a frivolous, giggling lassie who attracts all the young men of the neighbourhood."

The Earl laughed.

"I am quite certain you are neither of those types," he said. "But, whatever you look like, I am prepared to tolerate you as an Instructor, and allow you to torture me for just one week."

"That is a deal!" Vara declared. "I can only hope that when the week is ended you will be riding high as the most constructive and intelligent Chieftain the McDorns have ever known."

"That is a challenge!" the Earl exclaimed. "And one I accept!"

"Very well, then, My Lord," Vara said, "let battle commence!"

Vara left the Earl saying that she wanted to see to her unpacking.

Outside on the landing she found Donald, who had always been a special servant to the Chieftain.

She shook him by the hand and said:

"His Lordship has agreed to wear the kilt and all the other things that are appropriate to his position. I am sure you can find something for him until we can get a Tailor from Edinburgh."

Donald nodded.

"As it happens, Miss Vara," he said, "Ah've

found some that'll fit His Lorrdship as if they were made for him."

"I knew I could rely on you," Vara said.

As she left Donald, she knew he was smiling with delight.

She reached her bedroom.

It was one of the most attractive in the Castle because it was in a tower, and looked out over the bay.

The room was almost circular, with a four-poster bed that had been carved centuries earlier by local craftsmen.

It was many years since Vara had seen the room, but she had always thought it attractive.

She was delighted that it was where she was to sleep.

"I thought this was what ye'd like, Miss," Mrs. Ross, the Housekeeper, said. She had been at the Castle for over thirty years.

That everything ran so smoothly was almost entirely due to her.

"It is a lovely room!" Vara said.

At the same time, she realised that it wanted doing up, and that was another thing that the Earl would have to put in hand.

She put on a pretty gown for dinner, thinking it was a pity that her host could not see her in it.

It then occurred to her that he might prefer to dine alone because of his blindness.

But as she walked down the passage from her bedroom, Donald was there, waiting for her.

"His Lorrdship's takkin' dinnerr wi' ye in th' Dining-Room an' says that everything's t' be cut up forr him. An' Ah'm awa' noo t'tell the Piperr he's t'play roon th' table as is customary."

Vara was delighted.

She was quite certain this was another thing which, if omitted, would cause consternation to the Clan.

It was traditional in every Scottish Castle that the Piper played round the table at the end of dinner.

She went into the Chieftain's Room to find the Earl standing with his back to the fireplace.

He was wearing a kilt of the McDorn tartan, a Chieftain's sporran of white sheepskin, and a jabot of lace at his neck.

He looked exceedingly smart.

She could see that the skean-dhu had been pushed into the top of his stocking as she walked towards him.

As she reached him, she clapped her hands.

"You look magnificent!" she cried. "And your ancestors, whose portraits are hanging all around this room, are looking down at you with approval. I could see when I arrived that they were scowling."

The Earl laughed.

"I am quite certain that they violently

disapprove of what I think they call a 'Sassenach' taking their place in the Castle."

"Nobody here thinks of you as a Sassenach," Vara said quickly. "You have the blood of the McDorns in your veins, and that is what counts."

As she spoke so positively, she knew that the Earl was amused.

"This is the first time in my life that I have been taken to task about doing my duty," he said. "I have managed quite well up until now, but then, of course, I was in a civilised part of the world!"

Vara knew he was teasing her, but she said:

"Lesson One is that you hold your head higher and believe yourself to be more important than any other Chieftain in the whole of Scotland."

There was silence for a moment before she went on:

"And I suppose nobody has bothered to tell you that you are directly descended from Robert the Bruce—King of Scotland?"

"No-one," the Earl replied, "but I am sure it is something you will be telling me about before I am very much older."

"It is certainly my duty to do so," Vara answered.

"Dinner is ready, M'Lorrd!"

It was Donald, speaking from the doorway, and the Earl held out his arm.

"Now," he said, "ignominiously, as far as I am concerned, you have to guide me."

Vara slipped her arm through his.

"In the Opening of Act One," she said, "you certainly look the part of the hero, and, although I did not really expect it, you are behaving like one!"

The Earl laughed as she drew him deftly towards the door.

chapter three

VARA awoke in the morning with a feeling of satisfaction.

Last night had been quite different from what she had expected.

She had felt, in fact, that in teaching the Earl how to behave as a Chieftain, he had at least qualified for the position.

The dinner was excellent.

She noticed that Donald had the Earl's food cut into small pieces, and he ate with a spoon.

He managed quite well.

But she was perceptively aware that he was afraid of making a mess, and therefore ate very slowly and carefully.

The Cook, who had been at the Castle for

many years, rose to the occasion.

The food they ate was delicious, and the wine exceptional.

Vara was clever enough to refrain from talking about Scotland.

Instead, she encouraged the Earl to tell her about India and to explain the difficulties a Viceroy had to face.

He went on to other subjects, most of which Vara fortunately had read or talked about with her Father.

She knew that the Earl was surprised at how well informed she was.

She soon became aware as they were talking that the Earl was extremely intelligent.

When dinner came to an end, Donald said to the Earl:

"The Piper's here, M'Lorrd."

"The Piper?" the Earl repeated.

"It is usual," Vara said in a low voice, "that he should play round the table after dinner. Afterwards you must offer him a small dram of whisky in a silver cup which is kept specially for this, and he will thank you in Gaelic."

The Earl listened, and for a moment she thought he was going to refuse.

Then before he could speak there were the strains of the pipes being played in the distance.

As they came nearer, Vara noticed that the Earl was listening.

The McDorn who finally appeared through the door was, she knew, one of the younger Pipers.

She guessed why the Elders had chosen him for what was considered an important position.

Those who had attended on the late Earl were growing too old to turn out in the evening.

The Piper walked around the table three times, playing the tune of the McDorns, then *"Over the Sea to Skye."*

He stopped beside the Earl's chair.

Donald had put the silver cup down in front of him.

Vara reached out to guide his hand to it.

He took it up and handed it to the Piper who said:

"Stainte va!"

"I thought you played extremely well!" the Earl remarked.

Vara saw the young man blush at the praise.

Then he said several more words in Gaelic, drained the whisky that was in the cup, and spoke again in the same language.

As he went from the room Vara said:

"He was delighted that you praised him. He will boast about it all to-morrow, and the Elders will be pleased that you approve of their choice."

"I am haunted by these Elders," the Earl said, "and I presume that sooner or later I shall have to meet them."

"Towards the end of the week," Vara said quickly.

"In other words," he answered, "you are hoping that by then I shall not make too many *faux pas*, or disgrace myself in some way."

"I think that is unlikely, whoever you receive," Vara replied, "and I have an idea for to-morrow. But for to-night let us talk of other things than Scotland."

"Which, of course, is a great concession on your part," the Earl said.

Vara gave a little chuckle because she realised he liked to have the last word.

Then they went back to the Chieftain's Room.

The curtains were drawn and the fire, burning brightly in the hearth, seemed very cosy.

Vara guided the Earl to his chair.

As he sat there she thought that in the right clothes he looked exactly as a Chieftain should.

She could not help thinking it was a pity that none of the Clan could see him now.

As if the Earl knew what she was thinking about him, he said:

"Have I done anything wrong?"

"No, you get 'Ten out of Ten' for the way you behaved at dinner, and I am only hoping you will be as successful to-morrow."

They talked for about an hour.

Then Vara said she was going to bed.

*   *   *

Now, with the sunshine coming through the windows in her bedroom, Vara thought she must somehow entice the Earl into the open air.

At the same time, she knew that she would not be able to ride home as she had intended.

As soon as she was dressed she hastily scribbled a note to her Mother.

Then she asked Mrs. Ross if a groom could take it to her home.

"That'll be nay botherr, Miss Vara," Mrs. Ross replied. "It'll be done at once. Everybody in th' hoose was sayin' last night how smarrt His Lorrdship looked, dressed as he should be."

"We have Donald to thank for that," Vara said.

"Donald was pleased as Punch he had what was required, an' it's aboot time th' attics gave up their treasures, as ye might say."

Vara walked to the Breakfast-Room, wondering if the Earl would join her.

He might prefer to eat in his own rooms.

She was no sooner seated at the table than he came in with Donald, who guided him to his chair at the head of the table.

The Breakfast-Room was a small, round room, not as impressive as the Dining-Hall.

It was, Vara thought, easy for a blind man to find his way about in it.

"Good-morning, Vara," the Earl said. "I hope you slept well?"

"I always do in Scotland," Vara replied. "You will find the sea air, combined with that from the Moors, is very strong."

"I have found that already," the Earl said unexpectedly. "Instead of lying awake worrying about my eyesight, I slept."

"That at least is one good point for Scotland!" Vara remarked.

Donald, who was hovering beside the Earl's chair, asked him what he would like to eat.

"What is there?" the Earl enquired.

Before Donald could answer, Vara said:

"You must have a little porridge first and eat it standing."

"Why on earth should I do that?" the Earl enquired.

"Because it is a food that can be prepared quickly, and is itself a substantial meal," Vara replied. "You will stand because that makes it more difficult for an enemy to stab you in the back."

She stopped for a moment and then finished:

"You will be ready and alert to combat a member of any other Clan who might be approaching you surreptitiously."

The Earl laughed.

"Are you telling me that all the clansmen, now that the country is at peace, keep up these ridiculous practices."

"It is as traditional as the haggis!" Vara replied. "And for one week, whether you like it or not, you have to eat it."

"Very well," the Earl sighed. "I suppose this is one of the things I have to obey under our contract."

"Of course!" Vara asserted.

Donald produced the porridge in a silver bowl that had been used by several generations of McDorn Chieftains.

The Earl put the first spoonful into his mouth somewhat tentatively.

When he did not say anything, Vara knew that to his surprise he found it quite palatable.

After that he ate salmon trout from his own river.

As he did so, Vara told him how successful her Father had been the previous year.

"My Father keeps a record of every salmon he catches, its weight, the fly with which he caught it, and the pool he was fishing in."

"And who reads what must be by now a large number of books?" the Earl enquired.

"My Father pores over them in the seasons when he cannot fish. And you would be surprised how many other people find it interesting," Vara replied. "I suppose you know how to fish?"

"I used to go fishing in England on the River Avon when I was a boy," the Earl answered, "but nobody, except my Mother, was particularly interested in my catch."

"I will read you the record of some of the more sensational day's sport on your river," Vara said. "The books are all in the Library."

"So I have a Library!" the Earl exclaimed.

"Of course you have a Library, and a very fine one," Vara said. "It was added to every year with books which are of interest to the Scottish, until your Great-Uncle was too ill to read or be interested."

"I suppose that is another tradition you are expecting me to continue!" the Earl laughed.

"Of course you must," Vara replied, "and please, please, tell me that I may sometimes borrow a book from you."

The Earl threw out his arms.

"I suppose I should say, as they do in the East, 'Everything I have is yours.' But we Scots are too canny to say anything that might be misinterpreted!"

Vara laughed. Then she said:

"At least you are acknowledging that you *are* a Scot, and that is another step in the right direction."

When breakfast was over, the Earl went back to his seat in the Chieftain's Room.

Vara went to see Mr. Bryden and find out what she should read to the Earl.

"There are a great many papers I would like read to His Lordship," he said, "and there are also two callers."

"What do they want?" Vara asked.

"One of them is having trouble because somebody is stealing his sheep. The other is a woman who has just arrived to tell me that her roof has fallen in and she has no idea what to do. She has three children, the youngest being only two, and there is another baby on the way."

Vara was listening. Then she had an idea.

She told Mr. Bryden what it was, then ran back upstairs to the Chieftain's Room.

She thought as she entered that the Earl had a somewhat forlorn look about him.

As she walked towards him, he turned his head in her direction eagerly, as if he wanted to be active.

"There is something I want you to do," Vara said.

"What is it?" the Earl asked warily.

"I want to move your chair a little into the corner so that I can pull a heavy screen, which is used in Winter to keep out the draughts, around you."

"Why?" the Earl asked.

"Because I want you to hear two people who

have come to ask for your advice and guidance. They will not be able to see you, which I know is what you do not want them to do, but you will hear them. Then you shall decide what is to be done."

The Earl groaned.

At the same time, Vara thought that he was quite interested in her suggestion.

She made him stand up, moved his chair, then guided him to it.

The screen was a large leather one, with tapestry on one side.

Because it was heavy, she called Donald in to help her move it.

When they put it into position it completely concealed the Earl.

Vara went to the writing-desk on the other side of the room and sat down.

"Ask Mr. Bryden to bring up the man who has had his sheep stolen," she told Donald.

She was thinking as she waited how fortunate it was that people had come with their problems at this particular moment.

They were exactly the sort of difficulties that every Chieftain had to solve a hundred times a year.

The Shepherd who had lost his sheep was middle-aged, and dressed in clothes that were old and tattered.

But he held himself erect, and was obviously

extremely incensed by what had occurred.

Vara shook hands with him before she said:

"As I expect you have heard, His Lordship is not well enough to receive visitors at the moment, but if you will tell me your trouble, I will consult him and hope he can find a solution."

"T'at sounds fa-ir enough," the Shepherd said.

He talked with a very broad accent, and as he related his tale of woe, Vara was hoping that the Earl was listening and managing to understand.

What had happened was quite simple.

He had a large flock of sheep high up on the Moors.

During the last month one or two each week had been disappearing.

He was convinced they had not wandered away, but that somebody was stealing them.

He, however, was at a loss as to what he could do about it.

"Ah've tried watchin' forr them," the Shepherd said. "But Ah'm sure they must coome when 'tis darrk, an' Ah canna see, orr mebby they'rre spirrited awa' by Witchcraft."

"I think it is a case of their waiting until they know you are somewhere else," Vara suggested. "I will tell the Chieftain what has occurred, and see what he advises. In the meantime, while you are waiting, I am sure there will be a glass of Ale for you downstairs."

"T-at be verra kind o' ye," the Shepherd said, "an' Ah know th' Chieftain'll know what t'do."

Vara thought he was being optimistic.

When Donald escorted him downstairs, she went behind the screen.

"What solution comes to the Almighty Chieftain's mind?" she asked.

"I have not the slightest idea what to do about it!" the Earl admitted. "What do you suggest?"

"I think the most sensible thing would be for you to provide him with enough money to buy a dog, preferably two," Vara replied. "They can keep watch and alert him if any stranger should approach his sheep. At least it would be better than trying to stay awake all night."

The Earl smiled.

"Very well," he said. "If that is the advice I should give him, I of course agree, and I think it is a very sensible idea. How much does a dog cost?"

"No more than you can well afford," Vara answered. "And your Chief Shepherd can advise him where one, or two, may be obtained."

"I agree, and I am sure your judgement is as good as anything Solomon ever thought of, and will gain the approval of the Clan."

"You can be certain of that!" Vara smiled.

She then asked for the woman to be sent up whose roof had collapsed.

She was a harassed, worried-looking woman

62

whose husband was away at sea, as he was a Fisherman.

"Ah dinna ken what t' do, Lady," she said when she explained why she had brought her problem to the Chieftain. "'Tis Fate me wee bairns weren't killed. Bessie has a bruise on her forehead, an' Jamie's a cut leg. But, by the mercy o' God, they're alive!"

She had a great deal more to say on the subject.

Because Vara thought it was good for the Earl to hear this particular problem, she encouraged her to go on talking.

Finally, when the woman was breathless and her children beginning to fidget, Vara said:

"I am now going to take your problem to the Chieftain. If you will go downstairs, I am sure there will be something for the children to eat and milk for them to drink, and perhaps you would appreciate a cup of tea."

"That Ah would," the woman agreed.

Donald took them away, and Vara went once again behind the screen.

"What is your answer to this problem, My Lord?"

"It is obvious she must have somewhere to go with her children while the roof is being repaired," the Earl replied.

"That is what I was thinking," Vara answered, "and of course the repairs cannot be undertaken without your giving the order."

"Then tell Bryden to get busy on it at once," the Earl answered, "but they have to have somewhere to stay in the meantime."

"I think it would be a popular move if Your Lordship offered them accommodation in one of the outhouses at the back of the Castle. There must be a mass of unused furniture, beds, and other things they will require, stored away."

She smiled before she added:

"As you know, the Scots are very canny, and never throw anything away that might come in useful during the next hundred years!"

The Earl laughed.

"Very well. Tell them that is my decision."

"I will tell them, but you will have to listen to their gratitude," Vara said.

She did not wait for him to argue about it, but told Donald to send up the Shepherd.

When she told him what the Chieftain had decided, he gave what sounded like a hoot of delight.

"Why did Ah neverr think o' tat forr m'sel?" he asked. "Ma dogs are auld an' tired noo. Wi' two young ones, they'll hear and smell any stranger 'fore they can do any damage."

"That is exactly what the Chieftain thought," Vara replied, not revealing that it was, in fact, her own idea.

"Will ye thank His Lorrdship, an' tell him Ah

thank him frae the bottom o' ma herrt, an' Ah'll follow His Lorrdship wherever he leads us."

"I will tell him that," Vara said.

She thought what the Shepherd had said was very moving.

She hoped the Earl had understood him.

When the woman with the children was told what had been decided, she flung up her arms.

"God has herrd ma prayers!" she said. "An' ye can tell th' Chieftain He sent us tae him. May there be blessing on his head! May he always be kind tae his people as he's been tae us!"

She was still proclaiming her gratitude as Donald led her back down the stairs.

Mr. Bryden had been hovering outside to hear what had been decided.

He told Vara there was not only an outhouse available, but it was also furnished.

It had been used by visiting coachmen when the last Earl had entertained.

When he had gone, Vara went behind the screen and said:

"Now that you have introduced yourself to your Clan in exactly the way I have wanted you to do, everybody will be talking about it. I suspect tomorrow there will be a queue outside seeking your judgements, which they will be convinced will be entirely in their favour."

"I can see I am getting deeper and deeper into the mire," the Earl remarked, "and there will be no possible escape for me."

"Do you honestly think that to escape is what you want?" Vara asked.

There was a short silence before the Earl said:

"As you know, until I can see again, I have nowhere to go."

"Then you may as well make yourself useful here," Vara said. "But you cannot say that this has not been a successful morning so far."

As she spoke, she picked up the papers Mr. Bryden had asked her to explain to the Earl.

Donald moved away the screen and she started to read them.

There were certainly a lot of matters that required the Earl's agreement.

They included the fact that, since essential maintenance of the fabric of the Castle had been neglected, it was becoming infested with rats.

When she read this, Vara gave a little scream.

"If there is anything I really dislike," she said, "it is rats! Please give your permission right away for the Rat-Catcher to be sent for, and any holes to be bricked up."

"Of course that must be done," the Earl agreed sharply. "I cannot understand why Bryden did not have the sense to do something as soon as it became necessary."

"As your Great-Uncle is dead, Mr. Bryden would have been spending *your* money," Vara explained, "and he is too punctilious a man to wish to make any mistakes for which he could be reproached at a later date."

"Well, now he can get busy right away," the Earl said.

After that there was a new Gillie to be engaged on the river.

There were servants who were so old that they had to be pensioned off.

Then the coachmen were asking for new carriage-horses and for at least one of the carriages to be replaced.

"I only hope I have enough money in the coffers to pay for all this!" the Earl said. "Otherwise I shall be bankrupt and forced to sell the family treasures!"

"You must never do that!" Vara exclaimed. "They have been here for centuries!"

"Oh, so there are treasures?" the Earl replied. "I spoke without any knowledge that there were such things."

"Of course there are," Vara said. "There are goblets of great value which have been handed down from Earl to Earl. The silver, some of which is Jacobean, is exceptional."

She paused for a moment, and then went on encouragingly:

"And one day I hope you will be able to admire the gold candelabra which I was once shown as a little girl."

"I have some gold candelabra?" the Earl asked in surprise.

"Yes, indeed! They were used when the former Chieftain entertained important visitors, or when he gave a Ball."

She spoke a little wistfully, and the Earl said:

"Is that what you would wish me to do?"

"Why not?" Vara enquired. "There has not been a Ball at the Castle for fifteen years or more, and it would be very exciting if there was one."

"Are there enough local people to invite to one?" the Earl asked. "I was told that I had few neighbours."

"Of course there are some. They will fill their houses with your guests and will drive over in their carriages to the Ball. It will delight everybody—especially the Pipers."

"Are you telling me that I shall have to learn how to dance a Reel?" the Earl enquired.

"Of course our Chieftain should know how to do that," Vara replied.

"And all this is waiting until I can see again," the Earl said, "which you promised me I shall be able to do."

Vara did not reply.

She was saying a little prayer that he would, when he took off his bandages, be able to see.

Something inside her told her it would happen and that she was not just imagining it.

As she did not speak, the Earl said:

"Very well, I promise you that when I am no longer blind, I will give a Ball, and you shall be my Guest of Honour!"

"You had better wait until you can see me before you say that!" Vara answered. "If you are disappointed, you may feel ashamed of a 'Local Lassie' when your friends from London and other parts of England will be flocking to take part in a Ball which will be finer than any of those given in Edinburgh!"

"Now you are telling yourself Fairy-Stories," the Earl said. "I very much doubt if my English friends will want to come so far North, and, as you must be aware, I know nobody in Scotland."

"But they know you!" Vara argued. "Anyway, I am betting on a Ball taking place, and I shall start saving for a new gown."

"You are quite sure there is not one in the attics here?" the Earl replied.

Vara knew that he was teasing her because he had learnt where his kilt had come from.

She said quite seriously, however:

"I am sure there are dozens of gowns up there, and you might even make the Ball a Fancy-Dress party."

The Earl slowly shook his head from side to side.

"I am beginning to believe in this Fairy-Tale," he said, "but remember, first you have to give me back my sight."

There was a little pause. Then Vara said:

"I am praying that will happen . . . and I am quite certain the Minister is praying too."

She did not wait for the Earl to reply, but went to get ready for luncheon.

She was thinking as she did so that he was now talking about his infirmity without sounding despondent.

This was undoubtedly proof that she was making headway.

*   *   *

After luncheon, at which it was obvious the Cook had done her best to please, Dr. Adair arrived.

The Earl went with him to his bedroom.

When they had gone, Vara went to the window of the Chieftain's Room.

She looked out over the garden.

She thought when the Earl returned she would insist that he sit for a while in the sunshine.

There he could take in the fragrance of the flowers, the smell of salt from the sea, and the fresh air.

He would hear the seagulls and the cormorants, and she would describe to him how beautiful it all was.

"I have to make him see Scotland with my eyes," Vara told herself.

70

As she thought of it, she became aware of a little sound behind her.

She turned quickly to see a man standing by the fireplace.

She had not heard the door open, and she wondered who he was and how he had got in so quickly.

Then, as she moved from the window, he exclaimed:

"Vara! What are you doing here?"

It was then she recognised him.

It was Hamish McDorn, a young man she heartily disliked.

In fact, she had crossed swords with him just before she had left for England to look after her Aunt.

Hamish McDorn was the "Black Sheep" of the Clan, and her Father had refused to have him in the house.

He was unfortunately a relative of the late Earl.

He had gone so far as to claim when the Viscount was killed, that he should be declared the heir to the Chieftainship.

No-one, however, had paid any attention to him.

Vara had learned since she returned home that Hamish was still making preposterous claims before the present Earl arrived.

Now, as she walked towards him, she thought

that he seemed even more unpleasant than when she had last seen him.

She had known him ever since childhood.

His parents, when they were alive, had lived some way up the Strath.

They were a pleasant couple, and friendly with Lady McDorn.

It was only when Hamish was older and got up to every sort of prank that he continually found himself in trouble with the Elders.

Then Sir Alistair had said his daughter was to have nothing more to do with him.

"The boy is a bad lot!" he said when Hamish was sixteen, and he continued to say it over the years.

Hamish was now twenty-five.

All sorts of stories, some very bad, were told about him.

Vara was aware that all the more respectable members of the Clan would have nothing to do with him.

As she approached him now, he repeated:

"What are you doing here?"

"I was about to ask you the same question," Vara replied. "I expect you are aware that His Lordship does not yet wish to receive visitors."

"I know that," Hamish answered, "but I have as much right to the Castle as he has."

"That is nonsense, and you know it," Vara retorted, "and I see no reason why you should come here and upset him."

Hamish put his head a little to one side as he asked:

"Are you giving the orders here? This is something new!"

"I am here, if you must know," Vara said coldly, "to read to His Lordship because he is having trouble with his eyes. He has enough problems to cope with without your adding to them. So go away, Hamish, and do not upset him."

"I will not upset him," Hamish answered lightly, "and there is no reason for him to know, unless you tell him, that I am in the Castle."

Vara remembered she had not heard the door open.

"How did you get in?" she asked sharply.

"That is my business!" Hamish replied.

"It also happens to be mine because at the moment I am looking after the Earl. You should not have come without being announced, or walk about the Castle without permission."

Hamish looked at her with an unpleasant smile on his lips.

"If you think you can stop me," he said, "you will find it very difficult."

Vara had to admit to herself that this was true.

She was horrified at the idea that Hamish could move about the Castle without anyone being aware of it.

He was making himself at home in a way she knew would upset the staff and certainly the Elders, if they knew about it.

"Now, listen, Hamish," she said. "Just be sensible about this. His Lordship has said that he has no wish to see anyone, and I am trying to help him. So go away, and do not make things more difficult than they are already."

Hamish came a little nearer to her.

"What will you give me if I do what you ask?" he demanded. "A kiss?"

Vara stiffened.

"You are not to talk like that! You know that my Father has forbidden you to come to our house."

"I do what I want to do," Hamish boasted, "and I want to kiss you, Vara. I promise you, it is something you will enjoy."

"And I am quite sure it is something I will loathe," Vara countered. "I order you now to go away—at once!"

"What will you do if I do not?" Hamish enquired. "Call the servants and have me thrown from a tower? That would make a nice scandal and would certainly make the Earl more unpopular than he is already!"

Vara drew in her breath.

"What do you . . . mean by . . . that?"

"Everybody knows that he is blind, that he is sitting here hating the Clan, and is fed up because he has to be in Scotland."

Hamish laughed, and it was a very unpleasant sound.

"You may think he is interested in you, Vara, but I am told that he had the Beauties of London eating out of his hand before he went to India. And you can take it from me, they are a jolly sight more interesting than any Scottish Lassie."

"I am sure you are right," Vara said, "and now will you please go! His Lordship will be back at any moment, and, as you so rightly said, he has no wish for visitors."

She was hoping as she spoke that Hamish would move away.

Instead, he unexpectedly moved swiftly towards her and put his arms around her.

Vara gave a little scream, and fought against him.

But he was tall and strong.

She thought in despair that however hard she might try, she would not be able to prevent him from kissing her.

She struggled frantically.

Then to her relief the door opened.

At the sound of it Hamish released her.

The Earl came into the room escorted by Dr. Adair and Donald.

Vara put her hand to her breast, her heart beating violently.

It was the Doctor who demanded:

"What is going on here?"

"What is it? Who is in the room?" the Earl asked.

"I—Hamish McDorn—am here," Hamish replied, "and I am a relative of yours."

"A very distant relative!" Dr. Adair corrected him. "And certainly not someone His Lordship would be proud to know. Go away, Hamish, and try to behave yourself, as you have not done since you left the cradle."

"I am not taking orders from you!" Hamish said truculently. "Nor from anyone else, for that matter! I have a right, as every member of this Clan has, to speak to the Chieftain if I want to!"

He reached out, took hold of the Earl's hand, and shook it.

"I am delighted to meet you, Cousin Bruce," he said, "and I hope you will allow me to have a chat with you sometime. I can assure you, you will find me more interesting than the majority of the Clan, who still behave as if they had just come out of the Ark!"

He laughed a high-pitched, rather strange sound.

The Doctor gave Donald a meaningful look, as if to tell him to turn Hamish out.

Hamish, however, turned towards Vara.

"Our *tête-à-tête* was interrupted, my dear Vara," he said, "but it is something I will renew on another occasion. Take care of yourself."

He walked towards the door, then turned back to say to the Earl:

"Good-bye, Cousin Bruce. Do not forget me, for I shall be thinking of you and—who knows—it may prove advantageous to us both!"

He walked out of the room, and they could hear his footsteps going down the stairs.

It was then the Earl asked in a bewildered tone:

"Who is that man? What right had he to be here?"

"None whatsoever!" Dr. Adair replied. "I think you would be wise, My Lord, to do what the majority of the Clan do, and lock your doors against him. He behaves abominably, but by the 'skin of his teeth' has always managed to evade being sent to prison for his misdeeds."

"I am surprised at all this!" the Earl exclaimed as Dr. Adair guided him towards his usual chair.

He seated himself and said:

"Thank you for coming to see me, Doctor. You say there may be an improvement in the next few weeks."

"We can only hope so, My Lord," Doctor Adair replied.

He turned towards Vara and said:

"I should tell your Father that Hamish is giving trouble again. He dealt with him the last time he behaved intolerably."

"I know," Vara agreed, "but I do not want trouble at the moment when there is so much to do here."

"That is true," the Doctor said. "I will now leave His Lordship in your very capable hands."

He walked towards the door.

As he shut it behind him, the Earl said:

"Now, come and tell me what all this is about, Vara, and what that man was trying to do when we came into the room."

Vara gave a little sigh.

She had no wish to discuss Hamish with the Earl, or with anyone else for that matter.

But she knew the Earl was curious, and there was nothing else she could do about it.

chapter four

VARA had been in the Breakfast-Room for some minutes before Donald appeared.

"Ah'm afraid His Lorrdship's goin' t'be a wee bit late this mornin', Miss," he said. "He's had a bad night."

"A bad night?" Vara echoed in surprise.

She had much enjoyed dinner last night with the Earl.

The Piper had two new tunes to play, and she had persuaded the Earl beforehand to congratulate him warmly.

The young man had been delighted.

They had then talked for a long time about a number of subjects which did not concern the Clan, or even Scotland.

When she went to bed she had thought that the Earl was becoming far more human.

She was also sure that he was not as sensitive about his blindness as he had been when she arrived.

Now, as she waited for Donald's reply, she wondered what could have happened.

"His Lorrdship rang for me at three o'clock," Donald explained. "He was surre there was somebody in his room, but Ah found 'twas only th' rats scampering aboot in th' walls."

"Rats!" Vara exclaimed in horror. "Surely the Rat-Catcher is here by now?"

"He's herre, Miss, to be surre. But there's a great deal t'be done."

"Well, you had better see that he attends to His Lordship's rooms before he does anything else," Vara said, "and mine after that! I loathe and detest rats! They frighten me!"

"They were bad enough last year," Donald said reflectively, "but no as bad as they are th' noo."

Vara gave a little cry.

"Oh, I had forgotten!" she said. "How stupid of me! The Minister told me that one of the reasons he wanted me to come to the Castle was that Mr. Bryden and you were being woken in the middle of the night by His Lordship wanting something."

Donald nodded.

"Tha's true, Miss."

"Then I want you to put a bell outside my room," Vara said. "I understand they are the sort he can pull."

"They are," Donald confirmed, "and one o' th' footmen has put a cord along to th' room where Ah'm sleepin', which is near tae His Lorrdship. When he pulls th' cord th' bell rings an' wakes me."

"That is something I intend to prevent," Vara said. "So please do as I say and have a bell attached outside my room."

She smiled before she added:

"I am sure I can persuade His Lordship that if he must waken someone, it should be me. He cannot expect you or Mr. Bryden to be on duty both day and night!"

"Let's hope th' rats dinna wake him again," Donald said. "Ah'll speak tae th' Rat-Catcher noo. He's doonstairs in th' Kitchens."

Vara gave a little sigh.

She was well aware how large the Castle was, and if the rats were everywhere in the thick walls, it would be difficult to get rid of them.

"There's somethin' morre Ah think ye ought t'know," Donald said.

"What is it?" Vara asked a little apprehensively.

" 'Tis Mister Hamish, Miss. He's makkin' trouble doon at th' Harbour."

"What sort of trouble?" Vara asked sharply.

"He's bin tellin' th' young lads that His Lorrdship's had most o' his face blown away by cannon-balls an' he's so ugly he looks like some animal, an' tha's th' reason why he'll no let anybody see him."

"How can Hamish tell such lies?" Vara asked indignantly. "He saw His Lordship yesterday and knows perfectly well that only his eyes are affected."

"Mister Hamish likes makkin' trouble, ye ken," Donald said, "and o' course he's telling lies to anyone who'll listen tae him, an' sayin' His Lorrdship has not the right to be th' Chieftain, an' they'd be better off t'be rid o' him."

"I will speak to my Father about this," Vara said.

Then she had an idea.

"Have you a carriage, Donald, with a hood that can be taken down?" she asked.

Donald scratched his head.

Then he said:

"Aye, there's the one Her Ladyship used tae use. Ah think 'tis called a Victoria. It came up frae th' South, an' she enjoyed ridin' in it in th' Summer months wi' th' hood doon."

"Then have it brought round at noon," Vara ordered, "with the hood up. And send a groom immediately to my Father's house with a letter I am now going to write to him."

"Will ye be oot to luncheon, Miss?" Donald asked.

"I am going to take His Lordship to meet my Father and Mother," Vara explained, "but do not tell him so. I would rather do that myself."

Donald grinned.

"Ah ken fine ye'll do it betterr'n me, Miss."

Vara jumped up, and ran into the next room, where there was a desk.

Hastily she scribbled a note to her Father, saying that she wanted to see him about something important, and she was bringing the Earl with her for luncheon.

Then she added:

> "He has to have everything cut up
> very small, and he eats with a
> spoon."

She finished the letter, and signed her name with a flourish.

Addressing an envelope, she put the letter inside and took it to where Donald was waiting.

"Send a groom with this at once," she said, "and that will give them time to prepare something special for His Lordship."

"Ah'll see tae it, Miss," Donald promised.

He went from the Breakfast-Room.

About five minutes later the Earl appeared

with Donald guiding him.

He sat down in his usual chair at the head of the table and said:

"Good-morning, Vara. I hope you had a good night."

"Thank you, I slept peacefully," she said. "But I understand you were disturbed."

"I got to sleep again eventually," the Earl admitted, "but I dislike rats!"

"So do I!" Vara agreed.

She did not say anything else, but her eyes twinkled.

Donald gave the Earl his porridge and, without being reminded of her instructions, he stood to eat it.

Then he sat down again and enjoyed a substantial breakfast.

While he was doing so he said:

"I believe it is a fine day. What have you planned for me?"

"I have a surprise for you," Vara answered. "We are going for a drive behind two of the excellent horses you have in your stables."

"Driving?" the Earl questioned.

"I think you will enjoy it," Vara said. "But do not ask any questions because, as I said, it is to be a surprise!"

The Earl laughed.

"I think I am back in the Nursery," he said.

"That is the sort of thing my Nanny used to say to me."

"Mine did too," Vara said, "but in such a pronounced Scottish accent that you would not have understood!"

"Now you are being unkind," the Earl said. "I am beginning to understand most of what Donald says, and I even sometimes understand the footman, who lisps."

"I know," Vara said with laughter in her voice. "You are a very apt pupil, and I am sure you will win a prize at the end of the term."

"I shall now be wondering what that will be," the Earl said.

"That is what I will be doing too," Vara said. "You have everything a man could want."

There was a little pause, and she thought the Earl was going to say, "except my eyesight."

Instead, he said:

"I am interested in these stables to which you keep referring, and, of course, in the Castle itself. When you have time, I would like to make a tour of inspection."

"Yes, of course you must do that," Vara agreed, "but first I am sure that Mr. Bryden has some papers for you to approve. Then I will read you the newspapers so that you do not feel marooned in the 'back of beyond,' as you call it. And after that we will go driving."

The Earl did not protest.

When they left the Breakfast-Room Vara found as she expected that Mr. Bryden was waiting with a large pile of paperwork.

It mostly concerned things to be done on the Estate.

The most expensive item, however, was the Harbour, which had been neglected for years.

As she read out to the Earl what it was going to cost, she could not help thinking of Hamish.

She knew there were a number of young men in the fishing-village who had caused trouble before.

The reason was they had not enough to do.

She thought that was another subject that her Father might discuss with the Earl.

When it was nearly twelve o'clock, she went to her bedroom to put on her hat.

When she emerged she was carrying a short coat over her arm.

It was too warm to wear it, but she knew that a chill wind could suddenly come either from the Moors or from the sea.

But it would be good for the Earl to have some fresh air.

The sun was shining brightly as Donald guided him downstairs, and into the carriage.

Vara knew he was aware that the hood was closed, and he sat back in the corner so as not to be seen through the windows.

They drove down the drive and onto the road, where there were a number of cottages and a few shops.

As Vara had anticipated, there were people walking about who stared at the Victoria as it drove past.

She made no comment, however.

Only when they were out of the village did she start to describe to the Earl the beauty of the Moors.

Then they drove past a stream, and she told him how the salmon swam up it, and jumped the falls at the end to reach the Loch.

She thought the Earl seemed interested, but she was not sure.

Then, a little farther on, the coachman, as she had told Donald to instruct him, brought the carriage to a standstill.

"Why are we stopping?" the Earl asked.

"We are out on the Moorlands and we are going to lower the hood so that you get the fresh air," Vara replied.

"You seem to think there is something very special about Scottish air," the Earl said a little cynically.

"But of course there is," Vara declared. "It is good for your heart as well as your lungs, and your brain will also appreciate that it helps to create a host of new ideas which sooner or later you will want to put into operation."

"I think you expect too much," the Earl said, "and you will undoubtedly be disappointed."

"That is something I am determined not to be," Vara retorted.

The footman, having lowered the hood, climbed back onto his seat and the horses started off again.

"I now have a confession to make," Vara said, "and I hope you will not be angry."

"Do you expect that I will?" the Earl asked.

Vara drew a deep breath.

"I want you to discuss with my Father," she said, "what can be done about the layabouts in the fishing-village. They make trouble because they have not enough to do. My Father has said for years that some sort of work should be found for them, so I am taking you now to meet him."

There was silence.

Then, as Vara waited apprehensively, the Earl said:

"I was told that your Father is a very distinguished man. In what way?"

Vara told herself with relief that she need no longer fear that he would refuse to meet anyone, and she replied:

"Papa commanded the Black Watch until he retired. He was then Knighted for his part in a number of campaigns in which he distinguished himself."

"Then I would certainly like to meet him," the Earl said.

"You will, of course, realise that, as a McDorn, you would have been expected to join the Black Watch," Vara said, "which is the most famous Highland Regiment."

"I had no idea that was expected of me," the Earl replied, "for the simple reason that at that time I never expected to become Chieftain of the McDorns. There were two lives between my Father and the Earldom. I, therefore, concentrated on having what was the best in England."

"I have heard that," Vara replied, "but I think you missed something by not being in the Black Watch. It was designated a Royal Regiment over a hundred years ago, and they wear a red plume in contrast to the white one worn by other Highland Regiments."

"Why are they allowed to do that?" the Earl enquired.

Vara thought now he was really interested.

"It was authorised during the reign of George III," she said, "in recognition of a very daring exploit performed by the Black Watch during the French Revolutionary wars."

She paused, and as the Earl did not speak, she went on:

"Their tartan is black and dark green which they wear to indicate the Gaelic appellation of *Freicudan Du*, or Black Watch. Other regular troops wear scarlet coats, waistcoats, and breeches, and are therefore called 'Red Soldiers.' "

"I can see I have a lot to learn," the Earl remarked.

Vara instantly felt that perhaps she had said too much, and she lapsed into silence.

They drove on until the Earl said:

"Have you lived here all your life?"

"Of course," Vara replied. "My Father's family have owned our house for three hundred years."

"Then how is it that your English is so perfect?" the Earl enquired.

"Because I went to School in England. In fact, you will find that my Father has practically no Scottish accent, and my Mother none at all."

She did not say any more, thinking it would be a mistake to do so.

She was relieved when they arrived at her home.

The General quickly managed to put the Earl at his ease.

Her Mother spoke to him in her charming way, which everybody who listened found irresistible.

"We have been longing to meet you, My Lord," she said, "and it is a delightful surprise that Vara should have brought you here for luncheon."

"It was a surprise for me, too," the Earl said.

"We were hoping that you would want to

meet us," Lady McDorn said, "but I am sure Vara felt that we could perhaps help you in some way."

"I told the Earl, Papa," Vara chimed in, "that you have been saying for years that something should be done about the young men in the fishing-village. I heard this morning that Hamish is with them, and I cannot help feeling that he is plotting something outrageous."

"That would not surprise me!" the General answered. "And you are quite right, I have been saying for years that something should be done about those young layabouts."

"What did you have in mind?" the Earl asked.

At once they were talking animatedly about the different ways in which the young men could be employed.

The General saw that there were a number of trees near the Harbour which needed felling.

That could lead to boat-building, if they could get the right men as instructors.

It could prove a very profitable venture.

They talked about this all through luncheon.

Vara was listening.

At the same time, she was making sure that the food served to the Earl could be eaten by him without any difficulty.

The two men talked, trying to cap each other's suggestions.

Vara realised that the Earl for the moment had

stopped worrying about his disability, and was not thinking of himself.

'This has been a success,' she thought. 'Now perhaps he will not be afraid of meeting the Elders. It is most important that he should meet them.'

They talked until it was getting on in the afternoon, and the Earl thought it was time to return to the Castle.

Vara knew he had enjoyed being with her Father.

When she said good-bye to her Mother, Lady McDorn said:

"He is a charming young man. Surely the Doctors can do something about his eyes?"

"That is what we are hoping," Vara answered, "but apparently they simply do not know what is wrong."

Lady McDorn sighed.

"That is the story of so many ailments," she said. "I think perhaps he should go to London and see one of the top Oculists."

"He has done that already," Vara replied, "and they said the same as everybody else—that he could only hope time will prove a healer."

"That is poor comfort," Lady McDorn answered.

"I know," Vara agreed, "but perhaps now that he is not worrying about it quite so much, time *will* prove a healer."

"I shall pray for him," Lady McDorn said, "and I am sure, Dearest, you are doing the same."

"I am," Vara said, "but I am sure your prayers will be far more effective than mine."

Her Mother kissed her.

"You are a very clever girl," she said, "and I hope that the Earl will soon be better, because we miss you."

"It has been such a success for him to talk to Papa," Vara said, "and I feel sure he will want to come again."

She did not tell her Mother that their contract was for only a week.

She thought there was no time now for making explanations.

Her Father was helping the Earl into the carriage as she joined them.

She waved good-bye until they were out of sight of the house.

Then she said:

"It was a relief for Papa to talk to you about the fishing-village. It has worried him for years."

"He is right about it," the Earl answered, "and I can see that something will have to be done—and soon."

Vara wanted to give a little hoot of joy, but thought it would be a mistake.

Instead, she said quietly:

"I am sure that you and Papa will think up something which will not only help the young there, but will bring prosperity to many others of your people also."

"Are they very poor?" the Earl enquired.

"Yes, they are," Vara answered. "You have to find an outlet for the fabrics the women spin with the lambs' wool, and the fish that are caught in the sea."

"I am sure that can be organised," the Earl said after a moment. "Now that there is a train service, it should not be difficult to get the fish carried at least as far as Edinburgh."

Again, Vara thought with delight, he was thinking of how he could help his people.

They stopped on the way home to put up the hood.

When they got back to the Castle, Vara was sure that what they had discussed to-day would open the door to the Earl agreeing to see the Elders by the end of the week.

When they entered the Castle, Vara went up to her bedroom to take off her hat.

Then, looking out of the window, she gave a gasp.

In the bay there was anchored a large yacht.

She looked at it in surprise.

Then, having quickly tidied her hair, she hurried to find Mr. Bryden.

As she walked into the Secretary's room he rose to his feet, saying:

"I am sorry, Miss Vara. I did not know you were back!"

"We have only just returned," Vara said, "and I see there is a yacht anchored in the bay."

"It arrived about an hour ago," Mr. Bryden said, "and Lord Belgrave, who is a friend of His Lordship's, is waiting to see him in the Chieftain's Room."

"But will His Lordship want to see him?" Vara asked.

"I did not know what to say when Lord Belgrave was rowed ashore," Mr. Bryden said. "Apparently he knows His Lordship well, and is certain he will be welcome."

Worrying, Vara ran upstairs.

She went into the Chieftain's Room.

She thought perhaps the Earl was already there.

Instead, there was only one tall, good-looking man of about forty.

"Good afternoon, My Lord," Vara said. "I hear you have come to see His Lordship, and I am just going to find out if he will see you."

"He will see me, I am quite sure," Lord Belgrave answered. "I have a number of messages for him from his friends in India, and I am hoping that the affliction to his eyes is better."

"I am afraid not," Vara replied, "and because of it he has refused to meet anyone. But I will go and ask him if he will see you."

"As we have not been introduced," Lord Belgrave said, "you must tell me your name?"

"My name is Vara, and my Father is General Sir Alistair McDorn."

Lord Belgrave gave an exclamation.

"But of course I know your Father! He had a most distinguished career in the Black Watch."

"I have just taken the Earl to luncheon with him," Vara remarked.

She lowered her voice as she added:

"It is the first time he has met anybody outside the Castle since he came here."

"I can understand him feeling like that if he cannot see," Lord Belgrave said sympathetically. "But surely the Doctors can do something?"

"They have told him to keep his eyes bandaged for at least a month," Vara replied, "and are hoping the problem will solve itself."

Lord Belgrave made a helpless gesture with his hands as he said:

"That does not sound as if they have much hope! It is a tragedy, an absolute tragedy, that anything like this should have occurred. But of course, it could have happened only in India."

"H-how did it . . . happen?" Vara asked tentatively. "I thought when I first heard about it that it must have happened in battle."

"It was not exactly a battle," Lord Belgrave said slowly, "and in fact I was there at the time."

"Then tell me ... please tell me about it," Vara pleaded. "It is what I have been longing to know."

She glanced over her shoulder as she spoke, thinking the Earl might appear.

But a footman had closed the door behind her when she entered the room.

Lord Belgrave walked towards the window, and stood looking out at his yacht.

"It happened on the North-West Frontier," he began, "and I suppose it would be difficult for most people to believe it."

Vara raised her eyes to his as he went on:

"There had been a great deal of trouble the previous month, but it had quietened down and the Viceroy said he would like to visit the Fort. Of course, he intended to congratulate those who had beaten off the tribesmen who had been attacking our troops with Russian arms."

Vara nodded to show she was listening.

"We arrived there without difficulty, and the Viceroy talked to the troops in the Fort, who were delighted he had come. I accompanied him because I happened to be staying at Government House. He was attended by two of his *Aides-de-Camp*, one of them being Bruce McDorn, the present Earl."

Lord Belgrave paused as if he was looking back at what had occurred that day.

"It was after dinner," he continued, "when

we went out onto the battlements. There was a full moon, and nothing could have been more beautiful than the great rocks shining in the moonlight. The valley below us looked dark and mysterious."

Again he paused for a moment before he went on:

"And yet, as we knew, danger was around us. However, everything seemed very quiet, when suddenly three men sprang up out of the shadows to attack the Viceroy."

His voice sharpened as he said:

"It was so sudden and unexpected that they would have killed him if it had not been for Bruce McDorn."

"What did he do?" Vara asked.

"He acted more quickly than I could have believed possible," Lord Belgrave replied. "He shot the first two men before they could even raise their long knives. Then he tripped up the third man so that he fell backwards. At last a soldier, somewhat belatedly, raised his rifle and shot him dead."

"What happened . . . then?" Vara asked.

It did not sound as if the Earl had been injured in any way.

"It was then, while the Viceroy was now surrounded by soldiers, that suddenly out of the shadows—nobody could explain afterwards how he managed to get there—there appeared a *Fakir*."

"A *Fakir*?" Vara exclaimed.

"As you know, they are Holy Men who dedicate their lives to concentration and prayer," Lord Belgrave explained. "They are deeply respected by everyone in India, whatever their caste."

"I have read about them," Vara said quickly.

"The *Fakir* looked down at the dead men who had tried to assassinate the Viceroy, and then he cursed the hand that had killed them. I did not understand what he was saying, but I was told later that he used one of the most powerful curses known."

"A curse?" Vara murmured.

"He said," Lord Belgrave continued, "that as the men had lost their lives, so the man who had killed them should no longer see the world in which he lived, but only the darkness to which he had sent the dead men."

Vara gave a cry of horror.

"But that is . . . cruel! Unbelievably . . . cruel!"

"None of us took it very seriously at the time," Lord Belgrave said. "We went back to the Mess and had a drink, toasting Bruce McDorn, and the Viceroy naturally thanked him profusely."

"And then what . . . happened?" Vara asked.

"We all went to bed," Lord Belgrave said, "and the next morning we were told that McDorn had indeed gone blind. When we returned to Viceregal House in Simla, where we were staying, there was a telegram from England telling McDorn that his Great-Uncle was dead and that he was now the Earl of Dornoch and Chieftain of the Clan."

"That must have been a shock," Vara said.

"He realised he had to go home at once. But when the Doctors tried to treat his eyes, both in Simla and in Calcutta, they could only shake their heads and say that there was nothing they could do."

"It appears the Doctors . . . in London have . . . said the same . . . thing," Vara said in a low voice.

"It is impossible for us to understand how a curse uttered by a *Fakir* could work so effectively," Lord Belgrave said, "but very strange things happen in India! Some of their Priests and *Fakirs* have a power which Westerners simply cannot understand."

"There must be . . . something that will . . . cure him," Vara said desperately.

"We can only pray that is so," Lord Belgrave said. "On my way here, I was hoping that the situation would be better than when I last saw him in Calcutta."

"I am afraid it is just the same," Vara answered sadly, "and he is trying to shut himself away from the world, which of course is wrong."

"Indeed it is," Lord Belgrave agreed. "But I know that you, as your Father's daughter, will do all you can to help him. I have always been told that Alistair McDorn never knew when he was beaten."

Vara laughed.

"I hope I can say the same, and thank you for telling me what you have. Now I will go and see if His Lordship will see you, and I am sure he will."

She went to the Earl's room, and knocked on his door.

"Who is it?" he asked.

"It is Vara," she replied, "and as I expect you have been told, our friend Lord Belgrave is here."

"I do not want to see anyone!" the Earl said in a disagreeable tone.

Vara opened the door, and entered the room.

The Earl was standing by the window.

She thought he was wishing he could see the yacht which he had been told was lying in the bay.

He did not turn round as she stood just inside the room, and merely repeated:

"I will see no-one!"

"But Lord Belgrave very much wants to see you," Vara urged. "He has come a long way and you cannot be so inhospitable as not even to offer him a drink."

For a moment the Earl did not respond.

Then he said angrily:

"Why can I not be left alone? I have no wish to have friends telling me how sorry they are that I am blind."

"I am sure he will say nothing of the sort! He wants to give you news of India, and to tell you why he is here."

There was a long pause.

Then at last the Earl said with a sigh:

"Oh, very well! If I have to make a fool of myself, I had better get on with it. Take me to him. I suppose all it comes down to is that he wants to stay here."

"I should think he would be far more comfortable in his own yacht," Vara said, "but it would be polite of you to invite him."

The Earl did not answer.

As she reached his side he put his hand on her shoulder heavily, as though he wished to make her uncomfortable.

She walked towards the door with him moving beside her.

Then they were out in the passage, walking towards the Chieftain's Room.

"Dammit!" the Earl swore beneath his breath. "How long have I got to go on living in this accursed manner?"

It was then, as she heard the agony in his voice, that Vara had an idea.

chapter five

HAVING taken the Earl into the Chieftain's Room to meet Lord Belgrave, Vara slipped away to her bedroom.

As she entered she saw that the small case she had brought back with her from her home that afternoon had not been unpacked.

After luncheon, when the Earl and her Father were drinking a glass of port, Vara had gone upstairs with her Mother.

"I need two more evening-gowns, Mama," she said. "Have you a small case I can put them in?"

"Of course I have, Darling," Lady McDorn replied.

She paused, then added:

"It is a pity that nobody can see you in these pretty gowns."

"On the contrary," Vara said as she smiled, "the ghosts of the previous Earls look down at me with satisfaction. The present Earl cannot see the dining-room table, but it looks very glamorous with the gold candelabra and some of the beautiful silver, which I told the Earl was part of the family treasure."

Lady McDorn did not say anything.

Vara, however, knew she was wishing that her daughter could be surrounded by charming people and young men with whom she could dance.

"I suppose all Mothers are match-makers." Vara told herself.

She started to look in the wardrobe for the gowns to take with her.

Her Mother found her a small leather case.

Then she asked:

"Have you seen Mrs. Bryden, Darling?"

"Not yet," Vara replied. "I feel rather guilty about it, but she keeps to her rooms in her own tower. Of course I must go and see her."

"That reminds me—I have a book you can take her as a present. It is all about birds, in which I know Mrs. Bryden is very interested."

She hurried from the room.

When she had gone, Vara went to a drawer and took out a small revolver.

When she was fourteen her Father had taught her to shoot.

Her Mother had expostulated, saying:

"I think it is a mistake for a woman to learn to shoot."

"Women must be able to protect themselves," the General replied, "and as I have no son, Vara, if nothing else, must help me keep down the vermin."

Remembering the conversation now, Vara thought that if the rats came to her room, she would certainly shoot them.

She might even have to do the same in the Earl's room.

It was a small revolver, and quite light.

Her Father had made her practise on a target until she could hit the bulls-eye every time.

She knew however, it would upset her Mother if she knew Vara had it with her.

Quickly, she slipped it under the gowns in the case.

Even as she did so, her Mother came back with the book.

"Give this to Mrs. Bryden," she said, "and do not forget to thank her profusely for chaperoning you, even though you do not see much of her."

She smiled as she added:

"I am sure if we were in the South, they would think all this a very strange way to behave, but we have no alternative here in the Highlands."

Now, because her case had not been unpacked, Vara took the book for Mrs. Bryden out of it and also the revolver.

She put the revolver into a drawer in the bedside table.

Thinking this was a good opportunity, she walked the length of the Castle to its Northern tower.

She knocked on the door.

There seemed to be a long silence before the door was opened just a little.

A voice asked:

"Who is there?"

"It is Vara McDorn, and I have a message for you from my Mother."

Mrs. Bryden opened the door.

She looked at Vara somewhat suspiciously, then she said:

"Will you come in?"

Because she was curious, Vara did not refuse.

She followed Mrs. Bryden into what she saw was a very attractive and unusual room.

It was, of course, circular, and it had three windows looking out over the garden.

Outside was a small verandah with several bird-tables.

On them were a number of different birds picking at the food that had been laid out for them.

"My Mother told me that you were a keen

Ornithologist," Vara explained, "and that is why she has sent you this book."

She handed the book to Mrs. Bryden, who looked at it and said:

"That's very kind of Lady McDorn, and I'm sure it will be interesting."

"There are several species of birds on the bird-tables I do not recognise," Vara said.

Because she showed an interest, Mrs. Bryden told her what they were.

She pointed out specially some unusual species that she said came from the Northern Isles.

Vara thanked her for chaperoning her while she was staying at the Castle, and Mrs. Bryden said:

"My husband tells me that His Lordship's showing more interest in things than he did before, and we're very grateful to you."

"He has a friend with him now," Vara said, "and I am hoping very much that he will meet the Elders before the end of the week."

"That is what my husband is hoping too," Mrs. Bryden answered.

Vara thought it would be a mistake to stay too long, so she said:

"I had better go back and see if I am wanted. Thank you, once again, Mrs. Bryden, for your kindness."

"I'm afraid I've done very little," Mrs. Bryden said, "but I don't go into the main part of the

Castle unless I can help it."

"I am not surprised, when you have such a beautiful home here," Vara said as she smiled.

"By the way," she added as if on a sudden impulse, "is Mother MacKay still alive?"

"She is indeed," Mrs. Bryden replied. "I took her a wee young cormorant with a broken wing two weeks ago. She healed him in her usual miraculous manner."

"I remember visiting her when I was very young," Vara said.

Mrs. Bryden did not reply, so she said no more.

On her way back to the Chieftain's Room, Vara was thinking that tomorrow would be very crucial.

She did not mention what was in her mind until after dinner, because Lord Belgrave had dined with them.

He had obviously set himself out to entertain the Earl and keep him interested.

They talked of India, which to Vara sounded fascinating.

Lord Belgrave teased the Earl about his success with the ladies in Simla.

In case Vara did not understand, he explained to her:

"I must tell you, Miss McDorn, that in the hot weather the wives go up to the cool of the mountains in Simla while their poor husbands have to sweat it out in the plains. As there is usually a shortage of men in Viceregal House, the *Aides-de-Camp* have the most entrancing women hanging on their every word, and flirting with them quite outrageously!"

"I have read about Simla," Vara said, "and I would love to go to India."

"Perhaps one day you will have the opportunity," Lord Belgrave said, "and as Bruce will tell you, there is nothing more breathtaking than the snow-capped Himalayas."

The Earl said nothing, and Vara thought that perhaps too much talk of India made him more depressed than ever about his eyes.

She, therefore, changed the subject.

When they were leaving the Chieftain's Room, Lord Belgrave said:

"I am leaving very early in the morning for the Orkneys, and I must, therefore, say good-night, and good-bye."

He held out his hand to Vara, saying:

"It has been delightful to meet you. Please give my best wishes to your Father and tell him how much he is missed in the Regiment now that he has retired."

"He will be glad to think he is still remembered," Vara replied.

Lord Belgrave then said good-night to the Earl and thanked him for dinner.

Vara walked with him to the top of the

staircase, then went back into the Chieftain's Room.

"I found him a very delightful man," she said.

The Earl was standing in front of the fireplace.

"He is a great friend of the Viceroy," he replied, "but I am glad he is not staying long."

"I am glad, too," Vara agreed, "because I have something very important for you to do to-morrow. Lord Belgrave said how brave you were. I am just wondering if you are brave enough to undertake what may be a somewhat hazardous journey."

"What do you mean?" the Earl enquired. "What are you asking me to do?"

"I want you to visit somebody who I feel might help you," Vara replied. "But the only way to get there is on horseback."

There was a pause.

Then the Earl asked:

"You are asking me to ride when I am blind?"

"I will lead the way quite slowly, and I promise to make sure you will be in no danger, unless you fall off! All your horse has to do is to follow mine, and if there is any difficulty, I will take him on a leading rein."

The Earl was silent. Then he asked:

"Where are we going?"

"Almost to the top of the Moor above the Castle," she replied.

"Why? What for?"

"That is something I will tell you to-morrow. I want it to be a surprise."

"I suppose if I refuse, you will say I am a coward!" the Earl complained.

"I will not say that," Vara replied, "but I shall be hurt to think you do not trust me."

The Earl made a gesture with his hand.

"Oh, very well," he said. "If you think what you want me to do is important, then I will do it. But God knows what you are letting me in for!"

Vara did not say how pleased she was, but he must have known, because he added:

"All right, you have got your own way, and like all women, you want to be in charge instead of leaving it to the men."

"Now you are assuming what I do not feel," Vara said. "All I am saying is that what I am asking you to do is very important to *you*."

"And I have agreed," the Earl said.

"In which case, My Lord, I will now say good-night in case you change your mind."

Vara walked towards the door, and as she reached it, she said:

"I promise you that, however unpleasant it may be, it will be worthwhile."

When she left she saw that Donald was outside, waiting to guide the Earl to his bedroom.

* * *

In the morning Vara rose early, and went round to the stables.

As she had been told, there were some very fine horses in the stalls, and she explained to the Head Groom that she wanted the quietest horse for the Earl to ride.

She told him that she must have a horse which would not excite the horse he would be riding.

The Head Groom understood exactly what she wanted, and promised the horses would be at the side door at exactly two o'clock.

Vara had decided not to go in the morning.

She knew that Mother MacKay's amazing talent for healing often took time to work.

Ever since Betsy MacKay had been a tiny child, she had been aware of her healing powers which were sometimes described as "Witchcraft."

In almost every Clan there was a "White Witch" who was revered and consulted on every possible occasion.

Mother MacKay had been the Healer for the McDorns ever since Vara could remember.

She had been a strange girl who had seen ghosts and made predictions which, invariably, came true.

Because of this, she had gradually acquired a reputation which was known to everybody locally.

Her family farmed high on the Moors in a very isolated place.

If an animal was injured in any way, or a bird broke its wing, or a cow refused to give milk, they were taken up to Betsy MacKay for advice.

One winter a small boy lost his parents at sea, and there was no-one to care for him.

Betsy MacKay, who was then in her late thirties, had said that she would look after him.

He had joined her family in rearing the sheep.

When he was grown up, he built a small house for Betsy and himself, and it was there that she saw her "patients," as she called them.

Vara could remember when she had hurt her finger as a child by having it caught in a door.

Her Mother had taken her to see Betsy MacKay.

"Mother MacKay," as she was called later, had healed her finger by holding it in her hands and praying.

When Vara went to England, where they laughed at such things, she had almost forgotten about Mother MacKay.

Now, when Lord Belgrave told her that the Earl's blindness was due entirely to a *Fakir*'s curse, she knew this was the answer to her prayers.

If anyone could heal the Earl, it was not the Doctors or the Oculists, it was Mother MacKay with her miraculous powers, which she believed came from God.

Therefore, they were used only to do good, not evil.

The difficulty, Vara knew, was that the Earl, who was so English in his ways, might "pooh-pooh" the whole idea.

He might call it "superstitious rubbish" and refuse point-blank to see Mother MacKay.

She knew, therefore, that she had to be mysterious about it and get him there before he realised exactly what was happening.

She was certain it would be the last thing he would expect.

He would have no idea where they were going or what was happening until she had got him to the top of the Moors.

Fortunately, when morning came, there was a great number of newspapers to be read to the Earl.

Mr. Bryden had already got in touch with the contractors who were to repair the Castle, the Harbour, and a dozen cottages on the Estate.

Prices had to be approved, priorities arranged, and no-one could give the final word for work to commence except the Earl.

It was, therefore, luncheontime when Vara knew she had to tell him that the horses would be waiting for them as soon as they had finished.

She had been very careful to tell no-one where they were going.

She was afraid they might mention it casually to the Earl.

He might then refuse to go on what he would think of as "a wild goose chase."

Vara knew that he would not want anyone to see him if it could be avoided.

When Donald said the horses were at the door, she guided the Earl down a side staircase.

He realised the staircase was smaller and steeper than the main staircase, and asked:

"Why are we going this way?"

"It is a quicker way to the Moors and to where I am taking you," Vara replied. "We avoid the drive, the cottages, and the main road."

The Earl did not reply.

She thought, however, he was relieved to know he would not be seen with his bandaged eyes.

He was wearing a bonnet with a black cock feather at one side, caught by the silver insignia of the McDorns.

It became him, Vara thought.

She knew that once he could discard his bandages he would be extremely handsome.

"He is a very impressive man," she told herself.

Only as they were climbing at walking pace up a twisting sheep-track did she realise that if the Earl's eyes were cured by Mother MacKay, as she hoped and expected, then her services would no longer be needed.

It had never struck her before.

She was riding ahead, the Earl behind her, his horse quietly following hers.

Suddenly she knew that she did not want to leave him.

At first she had prayed for him and tried to help him simply because she knew it was her duty to the Clan.

But she had found she loved being with him. In fact, it was the most exciting thing that had ever happened in her life.

She wanted to go on talking to him, listening and advising him, as she had been doing.

Then she remembered how Hamish had said that the Beauties of London had all fawned over him.

Lord Belgrave had hinted at what a success he had been with the ladies in Simla.

The thought of it was like a dagger in her heart.

Vara knew then she had done the most foolish thing she had ever done in her whole life.

She had fallen in love with a man who was not the least interested in her as a woman, only as a Reader, and as someone who was useful in telling him what he ought to know about his own Clan.

"How can I be so idiotic?" she asked.

When the end of the week came, and if Mother MacKay had been successful, her job would come to an end.

She would then no longer have any excuse for staying in the Castle.

Then the Devil tempted her.

If she turned round now and went back, the Earl would remain blind.

Then she knew that would not only be a cruel action but also an evil one.

The *Fakir* had cursed the Earl when he had done only his duty in protecting the Viceroy.

If good was to triumph over evil, she could not be instrumental in trying to prevent it.

Ashamed of her thoughts, she prayed instead that Mother MacKay would be successful.

Somewhere in the blue sky above them, she thought, there was someone listening.

* * *

The sheep-track twisted and turned up the Moors.

They were high above the river, which now looked like a silver ribbon below them.

It was very quiet and very beautiful.

Vara thought that when the Earl could finally see his Estate he would know how lucky he was.

There was nowhere in the world quite as beautiful as Scotland.

Vara wanted to hear him compare it to the Himalayas and say that, because he was a Scot, there was no comparison.

He did not speak, but she had the idea that, because he was on a horse, he was enjoying himself.

She knew from the way he sat his horse that he was an expert rider, and her Father would have commended him.

There was now quite a long way to travel over an almost flat Moor before they climbed again.

Vara rode on, not talking, because she thought the Earl was taking in the scent of the heather.

He could hear the buzzing of the bees, and the croak of the grouse as they rose ahead of them.

Occasionally there was an eagle flying overhead.

Otherwise, there was just the whisper of the wind and the horses' hoofs.

Finally, she saw ahead of them the slope of a hill, and beneath it there was the small wooden house where Mother MacKay lived.

The farm that had belonged to her family was half-a-mile away.

The little wooden house which her adopted son had built for her had now mellowed with time.

There had grown up round it a few fir-trees and a small garden in front of it, still bright with flowers.

Vara rode on until just before she reached the

cottage where she waited for the Earl's horse to come alongside hers.

"We have arrived," she said quietly.

"You must tell me where," the Earl answered.

"I have brought you to see a woman known as 'Mother MacKay,' " Vara said. "She is an unusual person, and is one of the most important members of the Clan."

"In what way?" the Earl asked.

"She is known as a White Witch," Vara explained, "but she is actually a Healer."

She realised the Earl stiffened, and she said quickly:

"Everybody consults her when they are ill or in trouble. Mrs. Bryden brings her injured birds. Shepherds take her their lambs and ewes when they are hurt, and there is no one in the County who is more respected."

For a moment there was silence.

Vara was half-afraid that the Earl would turn his horse, and go back the way they had come.

Instead, he said quietly:

"Do you really think, Vara, that she will be able to heal my eyes?"

"I am certain she will!" Vara answered. "But the important thing is you have to believe in her healing powers in order to make them work."

Again, she was afraid the Earl might refuse to have anything to do with it.

Instead, he asked:

"Do we dismount now, or have we farther to go?"

Vara felt as if she had been holding her breath as she said:

"We dismount, and we do not need to tie up the horses. They will not go far."

Unexpectedly, the Earl smiled.

"If they do, it will be your job to catch them."

He swung himself from the saddle to the ground as Vara did the same.

They tied the reins to the horses' necks so as not to get in their way, then Vara went to the Earl's side.

He knew what was expected of him, and he put his hand on her shoulder.

She opened the small gate from which a tiled path led up to the front-door of the cottage.

The path was not wide, and, as if he sensed it, the Earl kept close to her.

They reached the door, and Vara knocked.

"Come awa' in," a voice said.

Vara murmured to the Earl:

"Mind your head—the lintel is low."

He did as he was told, and they went inside the cottage.

Sitting by the fire, over which hung a large cauldron like those the Gypsies use, was an elderly woman.

Vara knew that Mother MacKay must be very old by now.

She had, however, expected her to look the same as she had when she had first seen her.

Instead, Mother MacKay now had white hair, a very thin face, and her hands showed the blue veins of old age.

But her eyes seemed as bright and as sharp as they had been when she was young.

She looked at Vara and said:

"Ye came t'see me when ye were but a wee lass that had hurrt her finger."

"How could you remember that?" Vara asked. "But you healed me, Mother MacKay, and now I have brought you the new Earl of Dornoch, who needs your powers."

"Ah ken he's blind," Mother MacKay said quietly.

Vara thought it was typical of her that living so far away from the village she was nevertheless aware of what was going on.

Mother MacKay pointed with her hand to a chair opposite her own.

Vara guided the Earl to it, and he sat down.

"Ah'm right sorry t'hearr aboot Y'Lorrdship's blindness," Mother MacKay said, "an' ye must tell me how it happened."

Vara drew in her breath in case the Earl refused.

He said simply, however:

"I was cursed in India by a Holy Man— a *Fakir*—because I shot two men who were

121

attempting to kill the Viceroy."

"Ma spirits tol' me it was somethin' like that," Mother MacKay replied.

"Your *spirits* told you that?" the Earl enquired. "But I have not told anyone since I came here exactly how it happened."

"Ah thought ye'd come t'see me, ye ken," Mother MacKay went on, "an' Ah'll do my best tae rid ye o' the curse. Or, rather, those who guide me'll do their best."

"I cannot tell you what it would mean to me to be able to see again," the Earl said.

"Ye have tae believe an' let those who watch o'er us do theirr worrk," Mother MacKay said.

She rose from her chair and went to the window.

Now the small room was dark except for the light from the fire.

Mother MacKay then went to stand behind the Earl's chair.

"What Ah'm goin' t'do," she said, "is to tak' t'bandage from ye eyes, an' it's best ye keep them closed. When Ah touch them wi' the Light o' God, dinna try t'see."

She paused as if she was waiting for his answer, and after a moment he said:

"I will do exactly what you tell me."

"Verra weel," Mother MacKay said, "Ah trust ye tae keep ye'r wurrd."

The Earl had removed his bonnet as he came into the house.

Now Mother MacKay began to undo the bandages.

Vara could only faintly see her movements.

In some strange way she could not explain, the flames of the fire flickered and died down until there was only the glimmer of the embers.

She was aware, however, that Mother MacKay had undone the bandages and placed them on the table beside her.

Then she put her hands on the Earl's eyes.

There was no sound, but Vara knew she was praying, evoking the spirits in which she believed.

Suddenly in the darkness and quiet of the small room Vara became aware that there were not just three people there.

She could not explain it to herself, but she knew there were others present.

Her whole mind and body were vividly aware of it.

It was so real that she was as conscious of the spirits as she was of the Earl and Mother MacKay.

She could feel them vibrating round her as she shut her eyes and prayed for the Earl.

But she knew if she opened them she would see a light that was not of this world.

It was so intense, and yet so real, that she found it hard to breathe.

It came as a shock when in the same quiet voice Mother MacKay said:

"Noo the spirits ha' touched ye wi' their healing rays, but they say ye're no' t'open them 'til dawn is breakin' tomorrow morning."

"I understand," the Earl said.

Vara had opened her eyes.

She was aware that Mother MacKay was putting back the bandages over the Earl's eyes.

As she fastened them at the back, Vara went to the windows, and opened the curtains.

Mother MacKay had returned to the seat in which she had been sitting, and the Earl said:

"I do not know how to thank you. Will you tell me how I can do so?"

"Ah ken fine ye're goin' tae help the Clan," Mother MacKay said. "It is your help they need, and they need it urgently. The Chieftain must lead his people!"

"I am aware of that," the Earl said, "and when I can see again I promise you that everything will be made as perfect as it is possible."

"That's a' Ah want t'hearr," Mother MacKay said.

"But I would still like to do something for you personally," the Earl persisted.

Mother MacKay smiled.

"Ah'll be herre if ye need me. Ye have only tae

124

tell me what Ah can do for ye, an' a' Ah want is the approval of those who worrk through me."

"You are a very remarkable person," the Earl said.

He started to rise from his chair, and Vara went to his side.

Knowing from the sound of her voice where Mother MacKay was, he held out his hand.

"I do not know how to say 'Thank you,' " he said, "and to tell you that I do believe in you, and I know that you have helped me."

Mother MacKay smiled.

"Tha's a' Ah want tae hearr, M'Lorrd, but remember what Ah've tol' ye, dinna try oot ye' eyes 'til the morrow."

"I promise I will do as you have told me," he said.

He began to move to where he thought the door was, and Vara said to Mother MacKay:

"Thank you, thank you very much, and when I tell my Father what you have done, he will thank you, too."

Mother MacKay just inclined her head, but did not speak.

They went outside into the sunshine.

As Vara had expected, the horses were where they had left them, seeking out the grass amongst the heather.

She caught hold of the Earl's horse first and when she took it alongside the Earl, he swung himself into the saddle.

Vara mounted her own horse, and went ahead in the same way as when they had come up the Moor.

Only as she started back did she ask herself if the miracle she had prayed for would occur.

'No-one in the South would believe us,' she thought, 'but Scotland is filled with spirits. They fill the air, the sky, the rivers, and the Moors.'

In the far distance she could see the sea, and as they descended the hill there were the towers of the Castle.

"Please, please, God," she prayed, "let him see . . . let him be able to see!"

She knew it was the most unselfish prayer she had ever made.

chapter six

As they drew nearer to the Castle, Vara led the way through some shrubs and trees to avoid their being seen.

She wondered if this was the last time the Earl would have to hide from those who might see him.

By the side door there were two grooms waiting for their return.

"You are home," Vara said softly, so that the Earl would know they had reached the Castle.

He dismounted, and she helped him up the steps, and in through the door.

They moved up the side staircase in silence.

When they reached the landing, the Earl said:

"I want to go to my own room."

Obediently Vara took him to the door, and when he went inside, she went to her room.

There was no-one there, and she walked to the window to look out at the sea.

Once again she was wondering if to-morrow the Earl would see and she would have to go home.

She knew she would never forget this experience, the days she had spent helping him, getting to know him, then quite unexpectedly falling in love.

She had never imagined that love would come in such a strange way, or that she would feel it pulsating through her whole body so that she hardly recognised herself and her feelings.

'Whatever happens in the future,' she thought, 'I will never forget him, and I do not suppose I shall ever feel like this for any other man.'

She knew that her Father and Mother had fallen in love at first sight.

It had taken a year, however, for them to gain the consent of her Mother's parents to marry.

During that time they had neither of them looked at anybody else.

"That is what will . . . happen to . . . me," Vara had assured herself.

But for the Earl it would be very different.

She could imagine him going back to London when he found it boring at the Castle once everything was in order.

He would want to make everything perfect first.

She knew already from the way he gave out orders that he was an organiser.

He was very quick-brained.

She thought that, once he was no longer worried about his eyes, he would find a thousand things that needed doing.

'In that case, perhaps he will stay here for quite a long time,' she thought.

Then she laughed at herself.

She was only trying to invent possibilities of seeing the Earl.

Even if she returned home, perhaps she could come to the Castle occasionally to talk to him.

"I love ... him! I ... love ... him!" she told herself.

She felt that the waves beating on the shore below repeated the words.

She decided it would be tactful to stay in her room until dinner-time.

Then, wearing one of the new gowns she had brought with her from her home, she went to the Chieftain's Room.

The Earl was already there.

He had been dressed immaculately by Donald in the evening clothes of the Chieftain.

At the very sight of him, Vara felt her heart turn a somersault.

Despite his bandaged eyes she thought no-one could look more impressive or more handsome.

The Earl did not refer to what they had done during the afternoon.

They talked about a great many other things, including the Harbour.

"Have you come to any conclusion about what is to be done about the layabouts," Vara asked, "who are causing so much trouble?"

"I want to talk again to your Father about them," the Earl replied. "I feel that between us we will come up with something to occupy those youths and keep them out of mischief."

"You will be very popular with the Elders if you can do that!" Vara said.

"Ah, the Elders again!" the Earl exclaimed. "I have not forgotten that I have promised to see them."

"They are waiting for a summons to the Castle."

Vara thought as she spoke that that was another hurdle the Earl had taken.

Now there was only one really frightening problem to face.

It depended on whether or not Mother MacKay's treatment would restore his sight.

When they went back to the Chieftain's Room after dinner, since the Earl seemed disinclined to talk, Vara said:

"I have had a busy day, and I think now I will go to bed."

"For me it will be a long night," the Earl remarked. "To-morrow we shall learn if the answer is Yes or No."

Vara was about to walk towards the door, when to her surprise he rose from his chair and held out his hand.

When she placed hers in it, he said:

"I have to thank you, Vara, for all you have done for me. I know you have tried very hard, and I can only hope that our visit this afternoon will prove successful."

Vara's fingers quivered in his.

"I shall be . . . praying that to-morrow you will be able . . . to see," she said very softly.

"I shall be doing the same," the Earl replied.

She would have taken her hand away, but he raised it to his lips.

He actually kissed the softness of her skin.

"Thank you," he said again.

She felt as if the angels were singing because he had touched her.

Yet, she left without saying any more.

When she reached her bedroom she put her own lips against her hand where the Earl had kissed it.

She felt a little thrill run through her.

Now, when she went to the window, the stars were shining and there was a moon climbing up

131

the sky over the sea, touching the waves with its silver light.

It was so beautiful and so mysterious that she felt as if the Spirits of the Sea were sending out their powers towards the Earl.

Perhaps they, too, could sweep away the curse that had been put on him.

She stood looking and praying for a long time, before she undressed, and got into bed.

It was impossible to sleep.

She could think only of the Earl.

She worried agonisingly in case, when morning came, he was still blind.

"What can I say to him then? What shall I do?" she asked herself.

She felt the helplessness of a woman who loves a man and is unable to take his suffering from him.

What the Earl must be feeling was unthinkable.

How could he be sleeping, knowing that in the morning he would face either victory or defeat?

Vara tossed and turned until finally she forced herself to lie still and try to relax.

"What I must do is pray," she told herself, "and not think of my own feelings."

But, it was difficult not to do so.

However hard she prayed for him, there was always the question at the back of her mind.

Would this be the end of their association?

They had talked about his giving a Ball, and

she wondered if she would be invited to it.

He needed to know how to "oil the wheels," and her Father was a more experienced teacher than she would be.

He could choose teachers from experts who danced at the Highland Games, and were some of the best Reel Dancers in the whole of Scotland.

The same applied to so much else which could happen at the Castle.

The Earl had still not held the Ceremony in which the Clansmen kissed their Chieftain's hand and swore their allegiance to him.

Then, the Pipers would play from morning until night.

If the Earl was generous, there would be a stag roasting, home-brewed ale in great jars, and fire-works.

Vara could imagine the excitement not only of the young members of the Clan, but also of those who were older.

And no-one, she thought, would look more distinguished than the Chieftain himself.

There were so many thoughts turning over and over in her mind.

Finally she fell asleep, only to wake with a start.

She thought she heard a movement within the walls.

She decided it must be the rats.

They had awakened her and she sat up in

bed, feeling as she did so in the drawer of the bedside-table for her revolver.

It was not completely dark in the room.

Although the curtains were drawn, the moonlight peered through at their sides.

One curtain, where she had been looking out, was not completely closed.

Holding the revolver in her hand, she tried to see if there was any movement on the floor.

All the rooms in this part of the Castle were panelled.

She had always been told that behind the panelling there were secret chambers in which the women and children had been hidden in time of trouble.

She could no longer hear any sound.

She imagined the rats creeping along behind the panelling, and perhaps finding a hole through which to emerge into her bedroom.

She felt herself shiver at the thought of it, and her fingers tightened on the revolver.

"I must have dreamt it," she reassured herself.

She bent over to put the revolver back into the drawer.

Suddenly there came a clanging of the bell outside her door.

For a second she wondered what it was.

Then she remembered she had given orders that the bell-pull in the Earl's room should alert her, and give Mr. Bryden and Donald some rest.

She knew what had happened.

The rats had disturbed the Earl's sleep as well as her own.

He was ringing, as he thought, for Donald to come in and cope with them.

She jumped out of bed, ran across the room, and opened the door.

She was wearing only her nightgown, and had not stopped to put anything over it.

She was concerned only with killing the rats.

Outside the Earl's room on a table was a small oil-lamp which lit the corridor at night.

Similar lamps were to be found all over the Castle.

Vara had questioned the reason for it.

She had been told that the last Earl had considered the candles in their sconces were a fire-hazard.

Because there was so much wood used for the beams, the panelling, and the floors, he thought lamps were safer.

Vara stopped outside the Earl's bedroom door.

Transferring the revolver into her left hand, she then moved the oil-lamp as near as possible to the door.

She thought as she did so that she heard a slight scuffle.

Then, as she silently opened the door, she put the revolver back into her right hand.

At the same time, she lifted the oil-lamp from the table.

She went into the room and for a moment, as she looked towards the panelling, she could see nothing.

There was a slight sound from the bed, and as she turned towards it, she gave a horrified gasp.

There was a man in a kilt with his back to her lying on top of the bed-clothes.

Vara realised that the man in the kilt was holding a pillow over the Earl's face, and obviously trying to suffocate him.

The sound came again.

With a swiftness that was instinctive, Vara shot at the man lying on top of the Earl.

The bullet entered his thigh, and he gave a shriek of pain.

She fired again, hitting him again in the thigh.

He turned over, and fell with a crash to the floor.

As he did so, she saw that it was Hamish.

The pillow with which he had tried to suffocate the Earl fell on top of him.

Hardly taking in what was happening, Vara stood immobile.

She held the lamp high, the smoking revolver in her right hand.

Coughing and catching his breath, the Earl sat up in bed.

Vara took her eyes from Hamish, who was screaming and groaning and trying to grasp his bleeding leg.

Now she was looking at the Earl, whose eyes, unbandaged, were staring at her.

For a moment their eyes met, and they just looked at each other.

Then the Earl said in a voice that sounded strange and unlike his own:

"I—can—see! I—can see you—Vara!"

It was impossible for Vara to move.

She could only stand looking at him, and realised that she had been right.

He *was* the most handsome man she had ever seen.

"I can—see!" the Earl repeated. "And you are—exactly as I knew you would look!"

"You can . . . s-see? You can . . . really . . . see?" Vara asked in a voice that seemed to come from a long distance.

Behind her she heard someone come into the room, and as she turned her head, Donald asked:

"What's a'going on here, M'Lorrd?"

He had obviously heard the explosions from the revolver.

He was dressed in a thick dressing-gown, his white hair ruffled on his head.

He looked very different from how he did in the daytime in his kilt.

Before the Earl could speak, Hamish cried:

"Help me! Help me! I've been shot! I'm bleeding to death! Help me!"

"An' might Ah ask what ye're a' doin' in here, Mr. Hamish!" Donald demanded angrily.

"He was trying to suffocate me!" the Earl said. "Take him away, Donald. Lock him up, and he will be handed over to the Police to-morrow morning."

"Verra good, M'Lorrd."

Donald bent down, and, taking hold of Hamish by the arm, dragged him across the floor, and out of the room.

He left a trail of blood behind him.

As Donald shut the door they could hear Hamish screaming all the way down the passage.

Vara, however, was concerned only for the Earl.

She went a little nearer to the bed.

As she did so, she realised that by the fireplace there was an open door in the panelling.

This was how Hamish had entered the Earl's bedroom.

"Y-you are . . . not hurt?" she asked in a low voice.

"You came just in time," the Earl answered. "He had me pinned down, and I only just managed to ring the bell before it was impossible to move."

"And . . . you can . . . see?"

As she spoke she laid her revolver down on the bed, and put her hand in front of the oil-lamp to shade it.

"But . . . it is . . . not yet . . . dawn!" she exclaimed.

"The miracle you promised has happened," the Earl said. "I can see—I can see you quite clearly."

For the first time, Vara remembered that she was wearing only her nightgown.

As it was Summer, it was of an almost transparent material.

Impulsively she bent forward and, putting the oil-lamp on the table, extinguished it.

"Why have you done that?" the Earl asked. "Pull back one of the curtains. I want to see the stars."

Hoping it was too dark in the room for him to see her clearly, Vara did as she was told and pulled back the curtains.

The stars were still brilliant in the sky, and there was just a faint tinge of light on the horizon.

"It *is* nearly dawn!" Vara exclaimed. "You have kept your promise to Mother MacKay."

"The dawn of a new day and a new life!" the Earl said.

"I . . . I am so . . . glad . . . so very . . . very glad!" Vara whispered.

Fearing that the Earl was looking at her, she

moved back into the shadows and pushed the open panel to as she passed it.

"We will talk about that later," the Earl said, "and I have a great deal to say to you, Vara."

Vara reached the door.

"Try to go back to sleep," she said. "There is so much for you to do in the morning, and you must feel well and strong."

"I feel at the moment as if I could jump over the moon and swim across the North Sea!" the Earl answered.

Vara gave a little laugh.

"You will be able to do that. Of course, we must let Mother MacKay know that her Spirits have worked for you the miracle we prayed for."

"I think she knows that already," the Earl said surprisingly.

Vara hesitated for another moment.

Then, she knew that although she longed to stay, she must do the right thing and go back to her own room.

"I am thinking not only of Mother MacKay," she said, "but also God."

She went along the passage.

When she reached her own room, she knelt down beside the bed and prayed.

Only when she felt cold did she rise from her knees.

Then once again, ringing in her ears like the bell outside her door, was the question:

"Will he send me home to-morrow?"

She found it impossible, however much she tried, to sleep.

All she could think of was that the Earl would no longer be unhappy—no longer have to fight a lonely battle by himself.

He would be able to take up his position as the Chieftain of the McDorns.

But, would he hear the call of London and of all his friends whom Lord Belgrave had described so vividly?

It was then Vara wept.

She had until then kept her self-control.

She loved the Earl with all her heart and soul.

But she knew that he would never feel the same about her.

She told herself that to love him was as absurd as trying to touch the stars.

The Social World in which he lived would be waiting for him.

She suspected he might decide to spend at least half his life in the South, and come North only for fishing and shooting.

His was a world in which she had no part.

She cried like a child, the tears running down her cheeks.

Finally, she buried her face in the pillow.

Later, she told herself, she must behave with the composure and self-control which she knew her Father would expect of his daughter.

The Earl must never guess what her feelings towards him were.

She was certain he thought of her only as a "Local Lassie" who had been able to help him, and to whom he felt grateful.

Last night, in the excitement of being able to see again, he had told her she looked exactly how he had expected her to look.

But what did that mean?

After his blindness, he would have thought any woman was pretty.

"I have my pride!" Vara told herself.

She only hoped she would not betray herself before she was sent home.

chapter seven

VARA was asleep.

She was suddenly awakened when she heard someone come into the room and draw back the curtains.

With an effort she opened her eyes and saw that, though the sun was now well up in the sky, it was still quite early. She had not slept for long.

As the maid pulled the last of the curtains, she said:

"His Lorrdship tol' me tae call ye, Miss. He wants tae see ye as soon as possible."

Vara felt her heart give a throb of fright.

Could something have gone wrong?

Was the Earl suddenly blind again?

Why should he want to see her so soon?

She got out of bed, and washed quickly.

As the maid brought her her clothes, she said:

"Ye'd neverr believe th' goin's on, Miss. Ah've never hearrd anythin' like it!"

"Why? What has happened?" Vara asked, and again was frightened that something had happened to the Earl.

"Frae all Ah can mak' oot," the maid, who was obviously longing to gossip, replied, "Mr. Donal' locked someone, Ah think it werre Misterr Hamish, in th' cloak-room near th' front-door. He turrned th' key on him an' thought he'd be therre this morrnin', but when he went there he found th' window had bin broken in, an' whoever was there had gone!"

"Gone?" Vara exclaimed.

She knew it could mean trouble if Hamish had got away.

"Mr. Donal's in a proper stew aboot it," the maid went on. "One o' th' game-keepers was oot errly, an' says he saw some o' th' lads frae th' Harbour came an' broke th' window! Did ye everr hearr such imperrtinence?"

"They broke the window?" Vara asked, feeling she must hear the whole story.

"Aye, they did that. They took Mr. Donal's prisoner oot an' took him awa'. Ah think they've gone in a boat. An' Ah can tell ye 'cause

Ah've seen it mesel', th' cloak-room's covered in blood!"

The maid, who came from the village, was obviously enjoying the sensation she was causing.

"But . . . where have they gone?" Vara asked, thinking that was more important than anything else.

She had the feeling that perhaps Hamish was going to cause a great scandal.

Not only would she be involved for shooting him, but also the Earl.

"Th' game-keeper says he asked 'em what they were a-doin'," the maid was saying, "but he were alone an' he couldna do anythin' aboot them breakin' th' window."

"What did they reply?" Vara asked.

"They tauld him they were goin' awa' somewhere they wouldna be interrupted. I think they'll no be comin' back."

Vara felt relief sweep over her as the maid continued:

"An' a good riddance too, if ye ask me! The lads doon at th' Harbour are real bad, an' th' trouble they cause brings shame t' th' Clan!"

At least they had not harmed the Earl, and that was all Vara could think of at the moment.

She fastened her belt and took a quick glance in the mirror as she pinned up her hair.

Then she left the room without saying any more to the maid.

She ran down the passage, knowing that the Earl would not be waiting for her in his bedroom.

She expected he would be in the Chieftain's Room, but as she reached the landing, she saw he was standing there.

She hurried to him, looking anxiously up at his face, afraid that something had gone wrong and he could not see again.

But he was smiling at her.

"You have been very quick—for a woman!" he teased.

"You . . . wanted . . . me?" Vara asked.

Because he was smiling and because he looked at her with eyes that could see, she felt as if her whole being was singing with joy.

"Yes," the Earl said. "I have something to show you."

He put out his hand and took hers.

Then, he turned and walked not down the stairs as she expected, but along the passage.

She wondered where they were going.

They were moving into a part of the Castle she did not know.

When they had gone some way, they came to a short flight of steps which led up to a heavy oak door.

The Earl then went ahead, and opened it.

Inside, there was a stone staircase, and as Vara joined him he said quietly:

"Donald told me about this, but I wanted to see it for the first time with you."

Vara realised then that they were in the oldest part of the Castle.

It was the way up to the top of the oldest of the Towers.

This part of the Castle had been the fortress when the McDorns had fought off the Vikings.

Because they had been beaten, they had left the McDorn Estate alone and gone farther North.

There they had pillaged and plagued a not so determined Clan.

The steps Vara was climbing were very old, some of them broken with age.

The Earl, going first, kept hold of her hand.

Because he was touching her, she could feel little thrills of excitement running through her.

She was aware of how strong he was, and his vibrations seemed to reach out to her as they had always done.

At the same time, there now seemed to be something different about their message.

At the top of the steps there was another door.

When the Earl opened it, Vara saw they had come out on the roof of the Tower.

The battlements looked out over the bay and

there were the remnants of a very old cannon.

The Earl drew Vara towards the crenelated parapet.

The sun was now well up, and throwing a golden light on the sea.

The lights on the purple Moors on either side of the bay were, Vara thought, more beautiful than she had ever seen them before.

It was a long way down to the gardens, but she could see the flowers, and farther on, the low cliff above the sandy beach.

It was all so wonderful that she felt the Earl, too, must be spell-bound by it.

Then he said quietly:

"I brought you here to see what you have given me."

"It is all . . . yours," Vara answered, "and I have prayed that you would one day be able to see the beauty of Scotland."

"You made me see it when you described it to me," the Earl replied, "and now, as you said, I am 'Monarch of all I *Survey*'!"

"I am glad . . . so very glad," Vara said, "and I hope now that . . . you will . . . love Scotland . . . as I do."

The Earl turned his head to look at her.

Then he said quietly:

"You love Scotland—and what else do you love?"

Vara drew in her breath, feeling it was a question he should not have asked of her.

And yet, with his eyes looking down into hers, it was somehow very important.

She knew the answer, but she could not say it.

She tried to take her hand from the Earl's, but he would not let it go.

"Tell me!" he commanded.

"I . . . I cannot . . ." Vara whispered, "it might be . . . something you . . . do not . . . want to . . . hear."

"I want to hear it, and so, my Darling, tell me the truth," he demanded.

She felt as if the sunshine had suddenly enveloped her whole body.

Because she was so aware of the pressure of his fingers, she found it impossible not to give him her answer.

"I . . . I . . . love . . . you . . . !" she breathed.

"As I love you!" the Earl answered.

His arms went round her, and very slowly, he drew her closer and closer to him, as if he savoured the moment.

Then his lips were on hers, and it was a rapture that was somehow part of the sun, the sky, and the sea.

It seeped through her so that it was almost impossible to breathe, to think, or to move.

She knew only that the Earl was carrying her into the sky.

He kissed her until she could no longer think, but only feel, and know that she was enchanted to the point where she was no longer human, but a part of the beauty of Scotland.

The Earl raised his head.

"I Love you, my beautiful Darling," he said. "I fell in love with your voice the moment I first heard it."

"I . . . I did not . . . know that you . . . f-felt like that," Vara murmured, "and I was . . . so afraid that now . . . now you can see . . . you would not . . . need me any more . . . and you would . . . send me . . . away."

"Not need you?" the Earl exclaimed. "Can you imagine the agonies I have been through, knowing that sooner or later you might leave me, and I could not ask you to stay?"

"I would have . . . stayed . . . you know . . . I would have stayed!" Vara cried.

"Dancing attendance on a blind man?" the Earl asked. "That would be no life for a woman, especially someone as beautiful as you!"

"I *would* have . . . stayed with . . . you," Vara insisted, "for I, too, must have . . . loved you when I first . . . saw you . . . but I did not know . . . it was love . . . until yesterday . . . when I was taking you . . . to Mother MacKay . . . and . . . and I thought that . . . if she . . . h-healed you, you would . . . want to go back to the . . . beautiful women . . . who pursued you in London . . . or Simla."

The Earl laughed, and it was a very happy sound.

"Of course there have been women in my life," he said, "but, my Precious, and this is the truth, I have never been in love as I am in love with you!"

"Can it . . . really be . . . different?" Vara asked.

"So different that it is going to take me a lifetime to tell you how different you are, and how much you mean to me," the Earl replied. "You are a part of me, my Darling, just as I know now I am a part of Scotland."

He gave a short laugh as he said:

"I fought against feeling like this. I thought it could not be true—just part of my imagination. But I could not deny the call of my blood, and as you talked to me about the Clan and taught me how I should behave as their Chieftain, I found myself thinking of them, and knowing that I could not live without them or you."

He kissed her forehead before he went on:

"And, my Precious, you have told me how much there is to do, so we will get it done together."

"That is . . . what I have . . . longed for," Vara whispered, "but . . . I felt it could not be . . . true."

Her voice broke on the words, and she hid her face against his shoulder.

He held her very close, then gently he put his fingers under her chin, and turned her face up to his.

He saw the tears in her eyes and exclaimed:

"You are not crying, my lovely one?"

"I am ... crying from ... happiness," Vara wept. "I ... I c-cried last night ... because I thought I had ... lost you ... but ... now I am so ... h-happy that I do not know how to ... express it in words."

"Words are unnecessary," the Earl said as he smiled.

Then he was kissing her again.

He kissed her until the Castle seemed to twirl dizzily round them.

They were flying in the sky, higher and higher, until Vara felt that they were far away from the earth.

They were enveloped by the spirit of Scotland.

Then, below them, came the first sounds of the pipes as the Piper walked round the Castle to herald the start of a new day.

The music from the pipes seemed to join with the ecstasy within them.

The Earl drew Vara closer and closer.

She felt as if they were no longer two people, but one, indivisibly and for ever.

They were part of the Clan, and a part of

Scotland from which they knew they would never be able to break away.

Scotland was theirs, like their love, for all eternity.

ABOUT THE AUTHOR

Barbara Cartland, the world's most famous romantic novelist, who is also an historian, playwright, lecturer, political speaker and television personality, has now written over 590 books and sold over six hundred and twenty million copies all over the world.

She has also had many historical works published and has written four autobiographies as well as the biographies of her mother and that of her brother, Ronald Cartland, who was the first Member of Parliament to be killed in the last war. This book has a preface by Sir Winston Churchill and has been republished with an introduction by Sir Arthur Bryant.

Love at the Helm, a novel written with the help

and inspiration of the late Earl Mountbatten of Burma, Great Uncle of His Royal Highness, The Prince of Wales, is being sold for the Mountbatten Memorial Trust.

She has broken the world record for the last sixteen years by writing an average of twenty-three books a year. In the *Guinness Book of World Records* she is listed as the world's top-selling author.

Miss Cartland in 1987 sang an Album of Love Songs with the Royal Philharmonic Orchestra.

In private life Barbara Cartland, who is a Dame of the Order of St. John of Jerusalem and Chairman of the St. John Council in Hertfordshire, has fought for better conditions and salaries for Midwives and Nurses.

She championed the cause for the Elderly in 1956, invoking a Government Enquiry into the "Housing Condition of Old People."

In 1962 she had the Law of England changed so that Local Authorities had to provide camps for their own Gypsies. This has meant that since then thousands and thousands of Gypsy children have been able to go to School, which they had never been able to do in the past, as their caravans were moved every twenty-four hours by the Police.

There are now fifteen camps in Hertfordshire and Barbara Cartland has her own Romany Gypsy Camp called "Barbaraville" by the Gypsies.

Her designs "Decorating with Love" are being sold all over the U.S.A. and the National Home Fashions League made her, in 1981, "Woman of Achievement."

She is unique in that she was one and two in the Dalton list of Best Sellers, and one week had four books in the top twenty.

Barbara Cartland's book *Getting Older, Growing Younger* has been published in Great Britain and the U.S.A. and her fifth cookery book, *The Romance of Food*, is now being used by the House of Commons.

In 1984 she received at Kennedy Airport America's Bishop Wright Air Industry Award for her contribution to the development of aviation. In 1931 she and two R.A.F. Officers thought of, and carried, the first aeroplane-towed glider airmail.

During the War she was Chief Lady Welfare Officer in Bedfordshire, looking after 20,000 Servicemen and women. She thought of having a pool of Wedding Dresses at the War Office so a Service Bride could hire a gown for the day.

She bought 1,000 secondhand gowns without coupons for the A.T.S., the W.A.A.F.'s and the W.R.E.N.S. In 1945 Barbara Cartland received the Certificate of Merit from Eastern Command.

In 1964 Barbara Cartland founded the National Association for Health of which she is the President, as a front for all the Health Stores and for any product made as alternative medicine.

This is now a £600 million turnover a year, with one-third going in export.

In January 1988 she received *La Médaille de Vermeil de la Ville de Paris*. This is the highest award to be given in France by the City of Paris. She has sold 30 million books in France.

In March 1988 Barbara Cartland was asked by the Indian Government to open their Health Resort outside Delhi. This is almost the largest Health Resort in the world.

Barbara Cartland was received with great enthusiasm by her fans, who fêted her at a reception in the City, and she received the gift of an embossed plate from the Government.

Barbara Cartland was made a Dame of the Order of the British Empire in the 1991 New Year's Honours List by Her Majesty, The Queen, for her contribution to Literature and also for her years of work for the community.

Dame Barbara has now written 590 books, the greatest number by a British author, passing the 564 books written by John Creasey.

AWARDS

1945 Received Certificate of Merit, Eastern
      Command, for being Welfare Officer to
      5,000 troops in Bedfordshire.

1953 Made a Commander of the Order of St.
      John of Jerusalem. Invested by H.R.H.
      The Duke of Gloucester at Buckingham
      Palace.

1972 Invested as Dame of Grace of the Order
      of St. John in London by The Lord Prior,
      Lord Cacia.

1981 Received "Achiever of the Year" from the
      National Home Furnishing Association in
      Colorado Springs, U.S.A., for her designs
      for wallpaper and fabrics.

1984 Received Bishop Wright Air Industry
      Award at Kennedy Airport, for inventing
      the aeroplane-towed Glider.

1988 Received from Monsieur Chirac, The
      Prime Minister, The Gold Medal of the
      City of Paris, at the Hotel de la Ville, Paris,
      for selling 25 million books and giving a
      lot of employment.

1991 Invested as Dame of the Order of The
      British Empire, by H.M. The Queen at
      Buckingham Palace for her contribution
      to Literature.